CU00591812

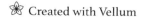

ALSO BY CATE LAWLEY

VEGAN VAMP MYSTERIES

Adventures of a Vegan Vamp

The Client's Conundrum

The Elvis Enigma

The Nefarious Necklace

The Halloween Haunting

The Selection Shenanigans

NIGHT SHIFT WITCH MYSTERIES

Night Shift Witch

Star of the Party

Tickle the Dragon's Tail

Twinkles Takes a Holiday

DEATH RETIRED

Death Retires

A Date with Death

On the Street Where Death Lives

FAIRMONT FINDS CANINE COZY MYSTERIES

Fairmont Finds a Body

Fairmont Finds a Dead Poet

LOVE EVER AFTER

Heartache in Heels

Skeptic in a Skirt

Pretty in Peep-Toes

LUCKY MAGIC

Lucky Magic

Luck of the Devil

Luck of the Draw

Wicked Bad Luck

For the most current listing of Cate's books, visit her website:

www.CateLawley.com

TICKLE THE DRAGON'S TAIL

CATE LAWLEY

1
------

ustin, Texas. December 1999

Getting my own apartment meant that I no longer had to live with my mother. Good thing, since she still didn't have a clue that magic was real or that her daughter practiced witchcraft. Mom's ignorance had proven awkward and inconvenient on more than a few occasions.

Moving into my new digs meant that my back was aching from shifting my thrift-store finds up two flights of stairs to my freshly painted—but decidedly chintzy—place. A girl on a budget had to settle for some chintz if she wanted her own place. And thrift-store shopping. No new furniture for me in the fore-seeable future.

Witches might make the big bucks, but I was

technically still a witch in training...and a grad student who hadn't finished her thesis, a part-time employee at my mentor's crystal shop, and a part-time makeup artist and girl Friday at my boyfriend's funeral home. A little hustle was helping to pay the bills while I finished my studies, both magical and academic.

Hustle also helped when it came to practicing witchcraft in an apartment complex filled with people. *Bunches* of people, none of whom had any inkling that magic existed. Hiding my witchy talents from nosy neighbors had just become that much harder.

I might be able to talk my way out of some flashy magic exposure, but it was best to keep the bangs, flares, and sparkles to a minimum and save myself the trouble.

"Star," Ben called out from the small balcony. He'd offered to set up my plants, and since they were heavy as heck, I'd agreed. Men were good for that sort of thing.

"Just a second. I'm almost done unpacking this box." The box containing my meager kitchen supplies, which would allow us to cook up some of the food we both were in desperate need of after hauling furniture all day.

"Yeah, hon, you're gonna want to see this. Now."

Uh-oh. Ben wasn't *that* guy. You know the one: bossy, rude, demanding. His tone meant trouble was afoot.

As I jogged the few steps from my miniscule kitchen to my balcony, I knew in my bones it was magic melodrama. I'd been working on giving Ben a view into my world—literally, using a combination of spells and charms—so now he could see some magic that other mundanes couldn't.

Also, if there was going to be a kink on moving day, it would be magical. Magic was fickle like that, picking the worst moments to go askew. At least, that was how it felt to *me*. My mentor Camille assured me it was all in my head.

I stumbled to a halt in front of the sliding glass doors.

All I saw was Ben pressed back against the glass. My redheaded hunk's tush might have temporarily distracted me, otherwise I probably would have noticed the stillness of his body more quickly. But once I did, it didn't take long for me to get a better read on the situation. I looked past him to find a visitor on my balcony.

The balcony door was cracked just wide enough

for me to slip through. I darted outside and practically squealed, "Marge!"

Maybe I sounded like a twelve-year-old getting her first pony. Not shocking. It wasn't every day that a dragon came to visit.

She lifted her chin from my balcony, gave me what I could only guess was intended to be a grin, then fluttered her long lashes at Ben.

"Uh..." Ben inched closer to me and whispered, "Do you see that? The scales and the teeth. And what's with the eyelashes?" He cleared his throat. "Is she *flirting* with me?"

Marge tilted her head coyly, which I took to mean, "Yes, I'm flirting with you, you hot hunk of man."

I wrapped an arm around Ben's waist. "I see her. Her name is Marge, and she's definitely flirting with you. Aren't you, Marge?"

Her lashes fluttered madly.

"She..." Ben quickly turned his attention from me to Marge. "Sorry. You understand us." Then he shook his head. "Of course you do. Marge, please tell me the neighbors can't see you. Star just moved in today, and it would be great if we could keep her here. Her previous living situation wasn't the best."

My mom wasn't *that* bad.

But then I tried to imagine what Mom would do if she found a dragon on her doorstep. Her reaction would be wildly different from Ben's calm acceptance.

My guy was the best.

Something niggled, something about Marge and my mom... A long-forgotten memory surfaced: my mom almost *had* found a dragon on her doorstep. I met Marge when I was sixteen. She'd turned up on the curb in front of my mom's house. She'd almost given me an anxiety attack, because I'd been sure I was about to be outed as a witch to my mother. But then Marge had acted so much like a sad, overgrown Labrador that I'd been completely enchanted by her and had forgotten my distress.

Actually, she was acting in a very similar fashion now.

Marge gave Ben and me a sad puppy-dog look.

But that sweetly mournful look didn't answer Ben's question.

"No one can see you, can they?" I cringed at the hopeful note in my voice. I didn't have much experience with the kinds of spells that hid large moving objects, so I hadn't a clue if one was attached to her right now.

Marge's eyes rolled up and to the left, and she looked about as sheepish as a dragon could look.

"I really hope that's uncertainty and not guilt," Ben whispered. "Because if she's visible and anyone can see her—"

"Yep. Big problem." I pointed at Marge. "Stay." Then I backed into the apartment, dragging Ben with me.

"Is she really three stories tall?" Ben asked as I pulled him into the kitchen.

"Uh, what? No. Maybe. I don't know. She has a really long neck. But, Ben, what the heck? There's a dragon on my balcony!"

"Isn't that my line?" He reached behind me for something on the counter. "Boyfriend freaks out and melts down when confronted by scaly monster with giant fangs. It sounds like a part I'm well qualified to play. One that's more appropriate for the person in the room without magic." He kissed my cheek and pressed my cordless phone into my hand.

Blinking at it, I shook my head.

"Camille?" he said gently. "Your mentor?"

"Oh! Right. Of course." I dialed her number from memory. I'd have come to that conclusion on my own...eventually. I was allowed a moment to collect myself when a mythical creature showed up on my doorstep. That was an official Big Life Event, not lessened one iota by the fact that the mythical creature was named Marge.

Camille's familiar voice filled my ear. "Camille's Crystals. How can I best brighten your day?"

"It's me." I licked my lips. "Marge is back."

A noise that sounded a lot like "eeep" chirped in my ear. My mentor was capable, powerful, and prepared for all eventualities. She also wasn't the squeaking type.

"Camille? What's wrong?"

"Uh, Marge is in a lot of trouble right now. Star, she can't be there."

Marge was tied up with some important memories. The passage of time might have buried them, but once jogged loose, I couldn't help but remember how important that day had been to me. Not only did my not-quite-adult self meet a dragon—a real-life, eyelash-fluttering, steam-breathing, purply-blue and green dragon—but Marge had also been the catalyst that had pushed me to accept the concrete reality of magic.

Heck, if a dragon showing up on your doorstep wouldn't convince you that magic is real, I'm not sure what would.

I quickly considered my options. "Let's say she's

not here. Let's say it was a drunk tequila moment.
I'm completely plastered. You know, moving is really
stressful and it makes a lady want to drink."

"Uh-huh."

"Right." I bit my lip and my gaze slipped to meet
Ben's. "So, having not seen Marge, maybe you could
tell me what kind of trouble she's in?"

In an emotionless tone, she said, "She's been
accused of frying Alistair."

My heart thumped erratically in my chest. "Riii-
ight. Gotta run. Bye, Camille." As soon as I ended the
call, I made a beeline for the box with the booze.

"Tequila? Is now really the time?" Ben asked.
Poor, innocent, uninformed Ben.

"Yep. No question about it, and you'll want one,
too."

Because there was a Marge manhunt underway
and probably a horde of vampires hot on her trail.
The trail that led to our balcony.

After I downed one shot, I poured another and
clinked with Ben's. "Marge has been accused of
toasting a very influential vamp in the area."

"Toasting?"

"Toasted. Fried like a squishy marshmallow."

Ben knew me. He knew I wouldn't let the masses,

vampiric or otherwise, get their murdering hands on my dragon friend.

And while I hadn't seen Marge in, well, a really long time, I'd still call her a friend.

"Right." That was all he said. No complaining, no "what if she did it," no hasty retreat out of my apartment or my life. "That's all right. We'll sort it out."

We. Which meant him and me, together.

Best. Guy. Ever.

But he did toss back that tequila shot and another one for good luck.

2

After being fortified with false, agave-flavored courage, Ben and I braved the balcony.

Small problem. And no, the neighbors hadn't spotted the giant purple, blue, and green dragon parked outside my apartment.

No, the problem was the absence of that gorgeous, lash-fluttering freak of nature. In the time it had taken me to call Camille and for Ben and me to down a few quick shots—maybe three or four minutes?—she'd disappeared.

Maybe we should have skipped the tequila.

"We could take this as a sign that she has it under control and doesn't need our help," Ben said.

I scanned the surrounding parking lot and the

empty field across the way. "Or the bloodthirsty horde got to her first. For all we know, dragon blood is extra tasty."

Ben didn't even flinch at talk of blood drinking. Total keeper, this guy.

"Hey, don't think that way." He wrapped an arm around my waist. "They'd have nabbed us, too, if that was the case."

Which made me laugh, because he wasn't wrong and it was both the most ridiculous and most effective way to comfort me.

"We have to find her, don't we?" he asked.

Did we? After some consideration, I landed on a different conclusion. "No. I don't think so. But we do have to find Alistair's killer."

"Hmm. What if it was Marge? How well do you know her?" He leaned back without letting go of me, giving me an intent look. "Maybe she did it. For all you know, this Alistair character deserved the marshmallow roasting he got and Marge was performing a community service."

Ben had been around the magical folk of Austin, Texas, long enough to have learned that vampires didn't generally represent the best of us.

If anyone deserved being roasted by dragon fire, it was Alastair. Pompous, entitled, arrogant, womanizing, all spot-on. There really weren't any positive adjectives for him. He used his position as one of the oldest, most connected vampires in the community to do whatever he liked. He was despicable.

Maybe I was being a *little* melodramatic, but I was allowed. Evil vampires might be after Ben and me, since Marge had fled here of all places.

Recalling the few times I'd met Alistair made my skin crawl. Even from beyond the grave, he gave me the willies. Vampires in general didn't produce the warmest of feelings, but Alastair was in a class all his own.

"No doubt he deserved whatever bad things happened to him, but I don't think Marge would have come here if she was responsible." I was pretty sure. Not that I spoke dragon, but Marge was a good egg. Camille had told me all those years ago when Marge first appeared at my house that she was a gentle giant. She only roasted what she ate, and she didn't have a taste for humans. I could hope that included persons who were formerly human. "I just can't believe that she would have led an angry horde of bloodthirsty, psychopathic vamps to my doorstep."

"Sociopaths." Ben opened the balcony door for me. "You told me vamps are sociopaths."

"Sociopaths who drink human blood on the regular. I think that qualifies as psycho."

"Fair enough. Speaking of, you want some dinner?"

I choked on a laugh. "You did not just use vampire dietary habits as a segue to dinner."

"Ah..." He gave me a sheepish grin. "I'm hungry. Besides, I'm pretty sure you have a plan. You might as well tell me about it while we make some food."

He knew me so well.

"I *do* have a plan." I flashed him a bright smile. "We're visiting the deceased's remaining family."

He sighed and picked up the bottle of Patrón. "Another tequila shot? I have a feeling I might need it before I hear this plan."

Once again, he wasn't wrong.

3

Visiting a dead person's family to interrogate them about the gruesome murder of their loved one posed a number of problems.

There's the grief. Are they even receiving strangers in their home? And if they are, are they capable of entertaining questions?

Then there's the question of delicate sensibilities. How do you talk about the deceased without triggering painful memories and endless tears?

But that was assuming the deceased was loved. Alistair was a vamp and his "family" were vampires.

First, vampires are sociopaths. When they're turned, their brains get fried. Something about the magic or the virus that turns them melts away their empathy. One theory is that it's an adaptation to hunting humans. Just like the huge fangs help to pierce a vein, the ability to disassociate themselves from their two-legged dinner allows them to attack and feed.

Sure, there's the occasional exception. Alex's friend Wembley, a wannabe surfer and all-around decent guy, came to mind. But generally, vamps are sociopaths. So the tears and the emotional land-mines I'd normally expect when calling on a recently bereaved person wouldn't be a problem in this case.

Second, vamps don't really have family. Not in the blood-tie sense. They can, but they usually don't because they live so long. I suppose someone could turn an entire family, but they'd all have to be susceptible to the virus that causes the transforma-tion. Since most of the human population is immune, that's not a very likely scenario. But either way, when it comes to vamps, "family" is typically defined through political ties and influence, not blood.

Who did Alistair leave behind that felt some allegiance to him? Well, these were vamps, so quite possibly no one. But who was politically allied with him and would feel that the attack on him was an attack on them? That could be a lot of vamps. Alistair was well connected.

Ben shoved his plate away and looked at the list I'd drawn up. "You're kidding, right? All of these people are going to be pissed that Alistair was killed? There are a dozen names here. I thought no one liked vampires, including other vampires."

I cleared the remains of our quickly constructed dinner as I replied, "I didn't say these people liked him, just that they'd be pissed. Could be they were closely allied with him, and they view his death as a personal attack. Could also be they had a particularly egregious complaint against Alistair, and now can't get satisfaction."

"Wait, you need to move those last ones to the suspect list. Wouldn't his enemies be more likely to kill him?"

"Ah, they're all suspects. These are the people closest to Alistair. All of them are potential sources, suspects, and the vamps most likely to crucify Marge if they get their hands on her."

Would they find her? Maybe she'd done a runner and had left town entirely. She could *fly*. It wasn't like it would be too terribly difficult to make her escape, especially if she still had some kind of glamor hiding her presence. None of my neighbors had piped up with reported sightings of a dinosaur or monster-sized lizard, so I had to assume Marge had managed some sort of glamor when she'd visited us.

"Hey." Ben touched my shoulder. "Let me do the dishes."

I turned around and realized he'd probably been talking to me while the water was running. I'd been so caught up in my worries for Marge that I'd zoned out. "Yeah, that's a good idea. What were you saying?"

He took the sponge from me and quickly washed the handful of dishes in the sink. "I asked if you were worried about your friend. But I think the answer is pretty clear."

"Ah. Yes. Very." I rested a hip against the counter and thought back to that first time I met Marge. "She's not exactly a friend. I've only met her once before, and it's not like we had a deep conversation even then."

Ben chuckled. "I'm guessing that might be difficult."

Smiling back at him, I said, "Talking to her is a lot like charades." The first time Marge and I met, she'd flashed those cute lashes at me. Marge was such a flirt. "I met her when I was sixteen. She'd just been cut loose very suddenly from her Djinn partner."

"You told me about them. The partnership allows the Djinn to communicate directly with the animal, and vice versa."

"Yeah. Marge's Djinn died suddenly. I'm not sure of the particulars. I was only sixteen at the time and had recently discovered magic. I'd been set up with Camille as my mentor only a few days before. It was an exciting time in my life."

"Wow. I bet it was, but also difficult. Your whole world was changing."

"Not really. It hadn't exactly sunk in. I was excited, but I didn't really get it. Magic, I mean." I blew out a sharp puff of breath. "But Marge arriving on my doorstep brought it all into focus. Meeting Marge was the moment that the idea of magic crystalized into a wonderful and terrifying reality."

"And you're sure that you're not confusing some of the feelings you have for magic with what you feel for Marge?" Ben picked up the bottle of Patrón. He lifted it questioningly, but when I shook my head, he stored it on top of the fridge.

"I get it." Twining my fingers with his, I said, "You

think I'm sentimental about Marge because it was a special moment in my life, and I'm sure that's partially true. That doesn't change the fact that she seemed kind back then, still did today, and that Camille has only ever had good things to say about her."

Ben raised his eyebrows. "When you spoke earlier?"

"She didn't say a word against Marge. She only said she'd been accused of frying Alistair. But when I was younger, she told me that Marge was harmless."

"Gotcha." A small wrinkle appeared between his eyes.

"What?" I knew that look. He had a question. He was curious by nature but didn't like to pry when it came to magic. He acted like it was this deeply personal thing, which I guess it was. "You have a question?"

"Yeah. Why you? When you were sixteen, I mean. Why your house? How was it, all those years ago, that Marge landed on *your* doorstep?"

I chuckled. "Well, I believe it had something to do with my newly acquired magic and maidenly virtue."

"Like a unicorn? She was drawn to the nearest

magical virgin?" Ben snickered. "That's not why she's here now."

"Right, Captain Obvious. I'm guessing she remembered me from the last time she was in trouble. I think she was here to ask for help."

"If you think so, you're probably right. I trust your instincts." Glancing at the table, where we'd left the interview list, he said, "But no interviewing tonight. We should probably get as much information about the people on your suspect list as possible, rather than going off half-cocked and—"

"We?" That was the second time this evening that he'd made it crystal clear I wasn't doing this alone.

"Yeah. Of course, 'we.' The funeral home is closed tomorrow, and I've already got someone to cover the phones and walk-ins on Tuesday, so *we* have two days to get to the bottom of this."

Two days. Vampires were slick on a good day. Yank them into a murder investigation, and they were bound to be impossibly slippery.

Actually, with all of Alistair's age and experience, I was surprised someone had gotten the drop on him. Especially someone like Marge. She didn't strike me as quite that conniving.

Someone, however, had been exactly that conniving. The question was: who?

"Two whole days to solve an impossibly difficult murder mystery, huh?" But then a huge grin spread across my face. "Wait, you have someone scheduled to cover for you on Tuesday?"

"Yep. Since you were taking off to move, I figured the least I could do was keep you company while you unpacked boxes and reorganized your bookshelf five times."

Riiight. I didn't think so. I knew exactly what he had on the brain. "You big perv. You were planning on spending all day Tuesday getting in my pants."

With a patently false look of innocence, he said, "I was planning to help you unpack." When I gave him a skeptical look, he said, "Okay, unpack *and* christen all of the apartment's flat surfaces. But can you blame me?"

I couldn't. That sounded infinitely preferable to visiting creepy, bloodsucking murder suspects. And the fact that he was still willing to take time off to help me, even though it would put him hip-deep in the muck of Austin's enhanced community, reminded me why I'd fallen for him in the first place.

That was hug-worthy.

Leaning back, so he could look me in the eyes,

Ben said, "I hate to ask, but...any chance you've been keeping up with your witch homework?"

Right. He would bring that up now. "Yes." Which was true, because what did "keeping up with" really mean? It was a subjective standard.

His forehead creased, but he didn't say anything. Wise man.

I caved and said, "Mostly."

"You've *mostly* been studying? What happened to becoming the best witch you could be? Your words, not mine."

With a solid push against his chest, I replied, "Moving, Ben, that's what happened. Moving, studying, and working two jobs."

But he wasn't wrong. I *had* said that. After practically having my rear handed to me during an investigation involving my ex-boyfriend Alex and a shady golem, I'd decided I'd rather be the one *doing* the butt-kicking. So I'd started to take my studies more seriously and had been working toward butt-kicking witch status...until life had intervened.

He stroked my cheek and very quietly said, "Maybe we shouldn't tangle with a bunch of vampires on our own. We can always call—"

"No." My response was a reflex. He wanted to call

Alex, because Alex was a powerful wizard, handy in a fight, and always had my back. But Alex was my ex.

Ben crossed his arms.

With a squinty-eyed look, I said, "Couldn't you be normal and be jealous of my incredibly hot ex?"

A smile twitched at the corners of his lips, but he kept a straight face. "Should I be jealous?"

I rolled my eyes. Alex and I were friendly...-ish. But that guy was a train wreck as a boyfriend. Any squishy, girlfriend-like feelings I had for him were long gone, and Ben knew it. What he might not know is that I'd never loved Alex the way I loved him. Ben was the One. I knew it almost as soon as I'd met him. But it still annoyed me to rely on my ex. "I just hate asking for Alex's help."

"How about Camille? You can ask your mentor, right?" When I nodded—because he was right; we needed help—he said, "Then call her, and see if we can swing by this evening. Get her to look at your list, and maybe she can send us in the right direction. And maybe you'll sleep better knowing more about what you're facing tomorrow."

"Good plan. And you never know, she may convince me that Marge doesn't need help."

"One can hope. If I can avoid knocking on the

door of a bunch of fanged fiends who want to suck my blood, that would be stellar."

He was joking with the bloodsucking comment, but only a little. I was pretty sure they wouldn't do that. In the light of day. With me along.

Pretty sure.

4

Camille lived in a quiet suburban neighborhood in south Austin. Every lawn was brilliantly green and every hedge trimmed just so. The yards looked bright and tidy, even at night.

"It never ceases to amaze me," I said as we passed another minivan, "that Camille manages to blend in here."

"It's south Austin. There's a hippie vibe in this area and she owns a crystal shop, so it's not too far a stretch." Ben pulled into her driveway and put the car in park. "Besides, there's no reason for them to suspect she's a witch. It's not like she dances naked in the yard under a full moon."

"That you know of," I mumbled, then opened

the car door and hopped out before he could ask too many questions.

He placed his hand on my lower back as we walked to Camille's front door together. After he knocked, he leaned close and whispered in my ear, "I heard that."

Whatever. Not like I joined her. That was Camille's thing. I wasn't into baring my lady bits to the night air. Not unless Ben was involved and we had some privacy, then I might reconsider.

The door swung open about a foot.

Ben nudged it with two fingers, and as it opened, we both looked down the hallway. Camille was noticeably absent, but Twinkles, Camille's maniacal cat, sprawled lengthwise across the entryway, blocking our access to the house.

As I inspected him, he grinned, flashing the tips of his fangs.

"You didn't do that. Did you?" I eyed him suspiciously. I'd had a look inside Twinkles' head not too long ago, and I knew what a selfish fluffball he was. Twinkles did only those things that made Twinkles happy and no more.

"We're not about to find Camille in the kitchen with a handful of Twinkles-sized bites taken out of her, are we?" Ben was looking at Twinkles with as much distrust as me. I was *pretty* sure he was kidding.

The cat's eyes practically sparkled with glee. Okay, maybe they didn't, but I would have sworn he seemed amused.

"Camille!" I called. "Holler if you're alive."

"Back here, darling." Her voice drifted into the hallway from the far reaches of the house. "I'm practicing my blind telekinesis."

Pointing a finger at Twinkles, I said, "Move it, buddy, or I'm stepping on you. I know exactly what's behind your cute, fluffy facade."

Twinkles narrowed his gorgeous green eyes and glared at me. Two, three, four seconds passed...then he leisurely rose, stretched, and sauntered down the hall.

As his fluffy bottom wandered away in no particular hurry, Camille appeared with a martini glass in hand. "What's keeping you?" Then her gaze dropped to Twinkles. "Naughty kitty. Have you been tormenting the guests?"

Contrary to her words, her tone was affectionate, and she reached down to scratch him under the chin.

"That cat is evil incarnate." I motioned for the martini. "Ben's driving. Hand over the martini."

"It's an apple martini, and this one's mine. I have yours in the kitchen, but you should apologize to Twinkles before you drink my delicious drinks."

Ben and I trailed behind as Camille led the way into her kitchen. The last time I'd been here, we'd cooked up a decoy body. That had been a useful skill to learn, but it also made me look at her kitchen table in a new, less favorable light.

Ben must have been having similar thoughts, because his gaze slid across the table, stuttered to a stop on the oven, and was followed by a look of mild panic. "You, uh, did some kind of magical cleansing in here after you cooked up that corpse, right?"

Camille smiled and nodded. "If that makes you feel better, Bennett, then I certainly did." She followed that obvious lie with a hearty sip of her martini.

Yuck. I didn't want to be thinking about faux corpses. It might be like baking bread, but it was still disgusting. "Where's that drink you promised me?"

Camille retrieved it from the counter, but then the evil woman held my precious beverage hostage. "So, about Twinkles... You're still pet-sitting for me over Christmas?"

Since I'd completely forgotten about that particular promise, she caught me off guard. "Ah. Yes. Where are you going?"

"I still haven't decided. But I'm overdue a vacation, so I'm leaving even if I have to camp on the side of the road. You know the Christmas shopping season is mad, so I'll need a break by the time we've powered through." She raised her eyebrows as she sipped her drink.

Ben pulled my suspect list from his back pocket, reminding me that we were here for a favor. Thank goodness for Camille and her generous nature. She was an amazing mentor. I snatched the list from Ben's fingers. Camille would give us all the good gossip just because she wanted to help me.

Most witches had a distinctly mercenary streak, but not Camille. She was incredibly generous, with me and her clients. And she was a total dark horse, which I adored. She wasn't fully appreciated in the witching community, since her particular brand of witchcraft—heavy on preparation and light on brute strength—wasn't as appreciated by the current regime. I smelled a hint of change in the wind, but it was a few years coming.

"Of course I'm still watching Twinkles." I leaned down to pet him, but he squeezed his eyes in what I was sure was a threat. After being inside that jerk's head, I wouldn't put anything past him. I casually withdrew my hand. Lifting the list, I said, "So, have you had enough booze to talk about vampires?"

She wrinkled her nose. "There isn't enough liquor to make that a pleasant experience. Just hand it over."

With a bland look, Camille perused the list of suspect-witness names I'd compiled. "Not bad. Except..." She grabbed one of the pens stashed in a jar next to her phone. After a few seconds of scribbling, she handed it back to me along with the pen. "Let's have a seat at the kitchen table, and I'll bring you as up to date as I can. Granted, they're not exactly my crowd. Consider what I'm going to tell you preliminary information."

Thank goodness for small favors. I doubted I'd still be mentoring with her if her social circle was filled with vamps.

She joined Ben and me after pulling a pitcher of premixed apple martini and a soda from the fridge. She handed Ben the soda and placed the pitcher equidistant between us. "I thought we might need additional refreshments."

Uh-oh.

I took my first look at her notes. She'd whittled

away my list of twelve names to nine. Two had stars next to them. "What are the stars?"

"Those are the vampires least likely to have been involved. Both of them have worked more closely with Cornelius over the last decade. Some vamps might like to play a long game, but that would be excessive."

Cornelius inspired mixed feelings. On the one hand, I wouldn't mind working for him when my apprenticeship ended. Basically, once I was a real witch.

Unlike Camille, I didn't have a huge stash of cash in my bank account. She might not be mercenary, but she was still a witch. She had mad bargaining skills, was business-savvy, and she knew how to turn her talents into profit.

I, on the other hand, was broke. Between my lack of savings and my massive student loans, gainful employment with an organization that paid top dollar for my magical skills should rank high on my goal list—my *long-term* goal list.

I'd avoided work there thus far, because I felt like so much of what happened in the Society was beyond my skill level, and I didn't mean magically.

The Society for the Study of Paranormal and Occult Phenomena might sound like a club for a bunch of ghost-hunting loons, but it was really a cover for the local enhanced community's governing body. The well-funded governing body that employed witches to perform all variety of tasks necessary for the functioning of a secret society. But the Society and I weren't always on the same page morally, ethically, and philosophically.

"You have that look," Ben said.

"What look?"

Camille chuckled. "The deer-in-headlights look you get every time Cornelius's name comes up. Stop worrying. There's time enough to decide whether you want to tie your wagon to the Society."

"Or not," I said.

"That's right. There are other ways for witches to make a good income. Look at Bernard and CeeCee and their thrift store venture." She finished her drink and poured another. "Or you could use your degree."

"Work in the mundane world?" My dismayed tone said it all. I hadn't meant to sound so crass. I was dating a man with no magic, after all. A great guy, whom I couldn't imagine being made better by anything, and that included having magic. "Sorry, Ben."

"Hey, it's okay." Ben lifted his soda can and

waited for me to clink my martini glass against it. "Of all people, you know I get it. You should do exactly what you want to do. You deserve that freedom."

We didn't talk about it much, but I knew that Ben didn't feel he had a choice when it came to his work at the funeral home. He was good at it, but it wasn't something he loved. I wasn't sure where his passion lay, only that he had a desire to do something else.

Kawolski Funeral Home had been in his family for generations, and he was the last Kawolski. Talk about feeling trapped by your job. Ben felt duty bound to ensure the business's continued success after his parents' retirement. Although given the lack of cash reserves when they'd left and the current state of the books, maybe continued *existence*, rather than success, was more accurate.

"At least all this running around with the crazy magical crowd is good for the business." I gave him a falsely cheery smile.

"True. And enhanced business only seems to be increasing. Good job, honey." He toasted me again.

"That's right! You've got the contract for enhanced body disposal in the greater Austin area." Camille shook her head. "I'm not sure how I could forget that. Good for you. It's also an excellent lead into the vamp community."

"Is there a body?" When she'd mentioned "fried," I'd assumed to ash.

"Oh, yes! Charred, but still body-shaped. Or so the grapevine says."

"Ugh." My stomach did a little flip. "That is so gross."

"You put makeup on dead people, and you think *that's* gross?" Camille asked.

"Oh, she thinks doing makeup for the deceased is disgusting, too." Ben grinned at me.

I almost denied it, but he knew me too well. "I don't mind dealing with the dead, but applying makeup is more complicated than I'd expected. That said, I've found that if I focus on giving the family the best possible version of their loved one that I can, it's really rewarding. I also give the deceased a nice pep talk while I'm doing his or her face, which makes the whole job easier. It's like I'm helping out a friend."

Ben arched an eyebrow.

"What? Okay, it's a little weird, but it works for me."

He tipped his head. "It does. You're good. I just

wouldn't go around advertising that you chat with dead people."

"It's not like they talk back."

Ben kissed my cheek. "Just let me know when they do, sweetheart."

"Please," Camille said with a put-upon look. "You two are disgustingly adorable. I'm happy for you, of course, but it's so...young."

Young? What did that even mean?

Her phone chirped, cutting off any reply.

Ben looked at it. "The phone just made a bird sound."

As Camille answered the phone, I explained quietly, "She spelled it to make a different noise when someone from the Society calls. This late, it has to be Cornelius or one of his enforcement guys."

"You mean like your ex?" he asked. And now he was just pushing my buttons. Alex and I got along just fine. So I didn't like relying on a guy that I used to live with, a guy with a total hero complex. Was that so wrong?

Camille motioned for us to join her and then flicked the phone gently with her nail, activating some prearranged spell. I've told her a few times she could buy a speakerphone, but she claimed the non-magical variety had too much static.

"You're on speaker, Cornelius." As soon as she announced this, she took a fortifying gulp of her drink. Cornelius had that effect on a lot of people.

"Bennett Kawolski?" Cornelius's clipped, sometimes British-sounding voice came across the line without a hint of distortion. Score one for Camille and the magic speakerphone.

"I'm here. How can I help you, sir?" Ben was a polite guy. He dealt with stressed-out and grieving people for a living, so he had a lot of practice handling delicate situations. Even so, I tensed. Cornelius had called specifically for Ben. Had hunted him down at Camille's, in fact. Something was afoot, and no matter how capable Ben was, I couldn't help worrying.

"We've completed our examination of the remains. Expect delivery tomorrow morning." Cornelius relayed the message as if it was commonplace for him to handle such matters, never mind the fact his assistant was usually the one who made body disposal arrangements for the Society.

Ben and I both looked at the clock on the kitchen wall.

Since Ben wasn't a part of this world and wouldn't be as comfortable declining, that left it to me. With another glance at the clock—midnight, and we weren't nearly done here—I said, "Right, ah—"

"I am aware, Ms. Lark, that the funeral home is not typically open on Mondays and that the hour is late, but you and your friend will accommodate us."

Camille held up her hand, silencing me. "Of course she will. They'll be there bright and early to meet Alex or Anton or whoever you've recruited to cart your carcasses around these days."

The silence that followed wasn't long, but it was impactful. When Cornelius spoke, he said, "Ten thirty. Any later wouldn't be wise."

"Thank you, Cornelius, I'm sure they'll be there promptly. Good night." And Camille ended the call. The woman had some gumption. I'd like to get to the point where I could hang up on Cornelius.

She flicked the phone again, and then turned to us with a glint in her eyes. "Opportunity has just knocked, Star. Pay closer attention in the future and maybe you'll hear it next time."

"What?" I was still doing the math and figuring that we'd maybe squeeze in six hours of sleep, but only if we were lucky.

Ben's warm fingers cupped the back of my neck and started to rub. "I think she's talking about the body. I'm thinking magical autopsy."

Camille nodded, and the little bit of tension Ben had been trying to work out of my neck quadrupled.

Brightly and with much too much fervor given the hour, Camille said, "You're up for a little magical slicing and dicing, aren't you, Star?"

5

"A magical autopsy," I said. "Didn't the Society just do one?"

We'd gathered at the kitchen table again. Mostly I'd stumbled blindly into the nearest chair and everyone had followed me. I hadn't ever done an autopsy. Well, naturally not the mundane kind. But even the magical kind. The one experience I'd had with an enhanced corpse, I'd only taken the barest of peeks with my magical sight and that had about knocked me out. It hadn't been a pleasant experience.

"Clarice is their go-to gal for autopsies." Camille shook her head. "Not her best skill."

That didn't sound like Cornelius. The man had exacting standards.

"Why don't you do them?" I knew she'd done some work for the Society, though she wasn't one of their regular contractors. And Camille would never provide substandard service.

Some of the mega-wattage, high-power witches might turn their noses up at Camille's craft, but I knew how powerful her potions, talismans, and charms could be, and how much juice she kept in reserve. Did anyone but me know exactly how powerful she was? I didn't think so. Camille was all about the slow burn, not the flash fire.

She made a tsking noise. "No. Autopsies are too political for me."

"Okay." That should scare me, but since I'd already decided to interrogate a horde of vamps, it only made me slightly more uncomfortable. The ship of caution had sailed, and my common sense was waving happily from the deck. "Why do you think I'd do any better than the incompetent Clarice?"

Ben snorted.

"Hey." I pointed at him. "I know you think I'm capable of all things impossible, but let's be realistic. A pro has already done the work, and I'm no autopsy pro."

"It's not a question of Ben's faith in your abilities,

or even mine," Camille said. "Clarice is not only less than adequate. She's also slow."

I shook my head in confusion. "It's only been a few days."

"A day," Camille corrected me. "Which is exactly my point. I do believe that Cornelius has just thrown an audition your way."

"But my apprenticeship isn't over yet!" Panic made my words sharper than I intended. I had so much to learn. No way was I ready to be cut loose from my mentor and wade into the depths of the Society.

"Calm down. Your apprenticeship is over when you and I agree it's over, and no sooner. And you can always turn down Society gigs. You know that, since you've done so in the past." Camille carefully tucked a strand of dark hair behind her ear. "That said... your apprenticeship has lasted longer than most." She blinked innocent, dark eyes at me. "And I would like to retire in the next five to ten years."

"Now you're just making fun." I leaned closer to Ben as his fingers dug into the base of my neck. Best. Boyfriend. Ever. Squinting at Camille, I said, "You know I just want to be prepared."

For everything.

Once Camille was gone—because I knew she

wouldn't retire in Austin—then it would just be me. I had some witchy friends, including Bernard and CeeCee, but there was no one I trusted as much as Camille.

All teasing gone, Camille's tone turned brisk. "Yes, well, we can discuss the trajectory of your apprenticeship later. For now, you have a list of suspects we need to chat about. You don't want to be too exhausted when you do your first solo autopsy tomorrow morning."

Don't think about autopsies, magical or not. Just don't.

Ben pushed the list closer to me, and I missed his talented hands immediately. Maybe I needed to work on my stress levels if I was relying on my guy to make sure I wasn't tied up in knots all the time. That was a task for next week.

"So, these two starred vamps? Good sources?" I asked.

Camille laughed. "They're working with Cornelius, but they're still vampires. Unless there's something in it for them, I wouldn't count on them."

I made a note to interview them last, since they were the worst suspects and no more likely to provide intel than the others. "That leaves six names. Bob Smith, Odette Martin, Lisette Wynter, and the terrible threesome: Max, Mike, and Mickey. Odette is his current..." Girlfriend wasn't right.

"Lover is the word you're looking for. Or mistress, since I'm certain there was no love in that relationship. She's a successful businesswoman in her own right, but the way Alistair treated her, you'd have thought she was nothing but arm candy."

"An ambitious, talented woman routinely treated with disrespect?" Ben tipped his head to the list. "I'd call that motive."

"In the land of vampires, I think that's pretty tame. If he tortured her every night..." But then I realized no vamp would put up with being physically attacked. "No, then she'd just rip his throat out —or try to. Maybe if he was undermining her business?" Either way, I made a note to see what we could find on her professional life.

Camille mentioned an advertising firm in which Odette held a majority ownership share and Alistair a much smaller interest. I wrote that down, too. But I wasn't really feeling it.

I returned my attention to the list. "Next up is Bob Smith, another of Alistair's business partners. Unlike Odette, Alistair had an interest in several of Bob's businesses."

"Bob Smith? Seriously?" Ben said. "Could the

guy not come up with a better name? It screams fake identity."

"To you," Camille said. "But that's only because you're expecting one. Bob, otherwise known as Robert James Miller Smith, hasn't used anything but some variation of his own name since he was turned a few hundred years ago."

Ben still looked skeptical. "Okay, Bob it is. As Alistair's business partner, he had to have intimate access, but what's the motive? What businesses, and how are they doing?"

"They have several," Camille replied. "Real estate, a used car dealership, interest in a medical practice, a private lab, and some other concerns."

There was definitely a theme. All of their businesses aided in underground, enhanced living in some way.

Ben must have seen it as well, because he asked, "Any chance that medical practice is a group of plastic surgeons?"

Camille nodded, which prompted me to review the notes I'd scribbled as she'd listed Bob and Alistair's various concerns. "Oh." I looked again. "Oh, this is disturbing. Not only can they skim blood from the bank—which is actually quite clever—but they can test human blood to see who lacks an immunity to the vampire virus and pick out their next victims. That's a step beyond clever."

Camille nodded, ticking her fingers for each of the businesses. "The plastic surgeons, to hide in plain sight. The used car dealership, because every good criminal or newly created identity needs access to wheels. The same for real estate. Come to Austin, newly turned vamp, and we'll provide you with a new abode, hassle-free but at great cost. And the list goes on."

Ben nodded, not nearly as bothered—or surprised—by this development as me. "It makes sense, Star. When there's an entire layer of society that doesn't age or ages slowly, that creates demand for certain kinds of businesses."

I laughed, but without humor. "Yeah, I get that. But something specifically about the vamps screening poor, unsuspecting medical clients really bothers me. It's a terrible invasion of privacy. Oh, and illegal. Super, crazy illegal."

"I'm more surprised that the witches haven't cornered the market on shady underground capitalism. Witches are terrifyingly proficient when it comes to making cash. Present company included but in a less terrifying, more ethical way." Ben grinned at Camille and me.

I didn't take offense—witches *were* notoriously business-minded, but not quite in this way. I paused as I tried to pin down the exact difference between Alistair's businesses and typical witch ventures.

By the time I hit on the major difference—witches were makers, and how had I not ever thought of us that way before?—Camille was already explaining. "Witches are entrepreneurs, sure. We can also be mercenary as a group, but we're not nearly as criminally inclined as vamps. We're more likely to invent something clever to exploit a need than to pervert the system to satisfy that need."

Wow. This was way too much introspection and philosophy for the middle of a night.

Focusing back on the murder, I said, "Can we agree that where there are shady dealings, there's a possible motivation for murder?" When Ben and Camille both agreed, I made a note that Bob was a strong suspect. "How about Tweedledee, Tweedledum, and Tweedledumber? The three Ms: Max, Mike, and Mickey. They seem to always be around, but I don't know their relationship to Alistair."

"They're all members of Alistair's goon squad and would have had ample opportunity to act against him. They were as close physically to Alistair as anyone would have been, but there are rumors of a loyalty contract."

"Oh." I fiddled with the pen, trying to decide if I should scratch them. "That would prevent them doing any harm to Alistair, depending on what kind of contract it was."

"If the contract exists. But for the purposes of discussion, let's assume there's no contract preventing them from acting against Alistair. What would their motivation be to harm their boss?" Ben asked.

Camille shrugged. "A grudge over Alistair's continued disrespect? They had to assume new names when Alistair took them on because he couldn't be bothered to learn their real names."

"Really?" I'd seen that in movies, where a butler or driver assumed the name of some long ago former employee—but that was fiction. Who did that in real life?

"A reflection of the privilege in which he was raised, I'm sure." Camille's tone was dismissive, but her words implied some deeper knowledge of Alistair than I would have thought her to have.

"So...Camille..." I raised my eyebrows. "Anything important you want to tell me about your relationship with the dead guy?"

She frowned at me. "No. Everyone knows he was one of the privileged back in the day. Most old vampires were. It required resources to hide and feed, so you were either wealthy, connected, or both if you were a vampire before the turn of the century." She sighed. "The turn of the *previous* century. I'm getting old, aren't I?"

Ben and I quickly disagreed. Not only because she really wasn't—or didn't look it; I had no idea how old she was in actual years—but I also had selfish motivations. I really didn't want her to retire yet.

"Back to the three Ms," I said. "I'll make a note that motivation is questionable, but means are plentiful. And Lisette? She seems to be a fixture in Alistair's life. She's in attendance and not far from him at every function I've attended."

Camille winced. "They do run in the same circles, but she's also his former lover and former business partner."

"Winner, winner, chicken dinner." I hopped up. "That's our first interview tomorrow...after we deal with the body." I pulled Ben out of his chair, where he was looking much too comfortable. "What's our best in with Lisette?"

"Her PA. Don't worry about it. I know her and

can get you an appointment. Get home, get some sleep, and take care of your business tomorrow morning at the funeral home. I'll call Suze, Lisette's PA, and get you an appointment. Just be sure to check in when you're done and get the details, because Lisette isn't someone you stand up."

Lovely. An autopsy I wasn't qualified to conduct that was an interview for a job I wasn't sure I wanted, followed by a date with a vamp who'd likely bleed me if I was running late.

Tomorrow was looking fabulous.

6

I grabbed Ben's mobile phone from the bedside table and answered it. No, I didn't usually answer his phone, but it was early, Ben was in the bathroom, and I hadn't exactly slept long or well last night. My brain was at about a third of its normal capacity.

"Stephanie?" came a confused voice.

Since I was Stephanie when I wasn't witching around Austin, I said, "Yes. Wait, Will? Is that you?"

"Yeah. Hey, I'm trying to reach Ben. There's a problem at the funeral home."

Which was closed, because it was Monday. Dang it. Will did the books, so he came in occasionally on Mondays. Who could blame the guy? It was quiet and he was less likely to run into grieving family members. Dead people he had no problem with, since he was in a completely different part of the building.

I glanced at the digital clock. Five after eight? No way Cornelius would show up that early and risk a civilian encounter or a mix-up.

"Is there a problem with the books?" I asked. I'd taken over some of the day-to-day bookkeeping, so I held my breath as I waited for Will to tell me I'd overdrawn the business account or double-paid someone.

"Oh, no, no. Nothing like that. You're doing great. You've got a good eye for detail. So, uh, Ben...?"

"He's in the shower. Can I take a message?"

"The shower? Oh! You guys... Right." He cleared his throat. "I, uh, didn't know you guys were an item."

"Yeah. So, is it an emergency?" If it wasn't the bank or a bookkeeping mistake, what the heck was going on? And please let it not be some magical problem I'd brought to Ben's doorstep.

Right about the time the butterflies in my stomach had reached a fluttering frenzy, Will said, "I was calling to tell him it looks like someone might have broken into the warehouse."

"What?" I hollered.

Ben rushed into the room dripping and disheveled, but staggered to a stop when he saw me still in bed and on the phone. "What's wrong?"

I handed him the phone.

"Hello, this is Bennett Kawolski." Some of the tension eased from his face. "Oh, hey, Will. Wait, what? The warehouse? Right. Thanks for calling." His jaw tensed and he said, "No. Don't call the cops. I'll head over now to check it out. If it's anything more than a little vandalism, I'll call the police. No, just leave everything like it is and go home. I don't want you there...just in case. Thanks, I'll be careful."

He ended the call and placed his mobile on the bedside table. When he sank into the mattress without saying anything, I started to get worried.

"What happened?" I touched his shoulder.

He shook his head. "The warehouse lock is damaged. Will didn't check inside, thank goodness. He didn't want to disturb anything, so he called me right away."

"Oh, Ben, I'm so sorry. You think someone's stolen some of your stock?" Because I helped with the books, I knew exactly how much Kawolski Funeral Home couldn't afford to lose any of the expensive caskets that were stored in the warehouse.

Even with insurance, there were deductibles. Any theft would have a serious impact on the business.

He arched an eyebrow. "No. I'm pretty sure the caskets are safe. Will also told me that it looked like some kids had been messing around in the field next to the funeral home. As he drove in, he saw some scorch marks that he guessed were caused by fireworks or small fires."

"Marge." I rolled out of bed so fast my head spun. "Let me just throw some clothes on."

"Yeah. Hurry."

And in five minutes, we were out the door and on the way to Kawolski Funeral Home.

The drive seemed to last forever. It didn't help that we were both consumed by our own thoughts and barely spoke a word for the duration.

As Ben pulled into the funeral home's long drive, we spotted the first of the scorch marks. They were only visible from the driveway, not from the main road.

"I count seven," Ben said. "You think it's some kind of code?"

"Or Marge hunting rabbits." When Ben shot me a funny look, I grimaced. "Sorry. I really don't know."

"Can you tell for sure if they're made from dragon fire?"

"Oh, shoot. Back up and let me get a look. If I use my sight, I can tell you if they have a magical origin." By "sight," I meant the magical variety, the kind that required me to use my inner spark of magic more than my eyes. I'd been practicing regularly up until Halloween, but with all the apartment hunting, then the big move, I hadn't been so diligent. "That's close enough."

Ben parked on the grassy verge about ten feet from a streak of scorched grass. The shape and symmetry of the marks, the dew on the grass, and the fact we'd been visited by a fire-breathing Marge yesterday all told me these marks weren't from fireworks.

But I still had to check. "I can do this."

Ben chuckled. "What were you telling me yesterday about not keeping up with your studies?" I groaned, and he quickly added, "Hey, I'm kidding. You've got this. You're incredibly talented, and I'm constantly impressed by what you can do." He scanned the funeral home's parking lot and looked behind us down the drive. "And it looks like you're the most qualified witch within at least a hundred-foot radius, so it's all you."

"Cute. And it's more like ten miles." I opened the door. "Stay here. It shouldn't take me very long."

I hoped.

Magical sight required concentration. I didn't know what it was like for other witches—Camille said everyone used magic in slightly different ways —but for me, I needed to tune out the world and focus. Thankfully, the birds and crickets weren't too obnoxious this morning. As I homed in on the black slash in the weedy grass, I saw flashes of brilliant orange coming off the mark in waves.

And that presented a conundrum.

"Well?" Ben asked as I climbed back into the passenger seat of his sedan.

I pointed up the drive. Once the car was rolling again, I said, "Definitely created using magic. But small problem. Dragons aren't actually all that common."

"And?"

"And I haven't a clue what dragon fire or dragon magic looks like, or how I'm supposed to tell if a dragon or a magically directed lightning strike made those marks."

Ben laughed. "Lightning? That's what you've got?"

That made me want to thwack him, but I refrained, since he was still driving.

"If this autopsy is Cornelius's way of interviewing

you," Ben said, "and you haven't a clue how to spot the use of dragon fire, I have to wonder if he really doesn't want you working with his people. He's handicapping you from the get-go."

I shrugged. Did it matter? Did I even want a job with the Society? "On the upside, I could tell magic was involved. I didn't recognize the *type* of magic, but magic was used."

Ben pulled into his regular parking spot. "Process of elimination, then. You know what didn't make those marks. Whatever remains, however long the list, is what you work with. And you do the same with the body."

"Right, Mr. Logical. I got it, it's just a little over-whelming, given my lack of firsthand knowledge. But let's go see if Marge paid you a visit last night. If we can find evidence of her presence, then I've got a tie between her and those marks out front."

The warehouse wasn't more than twenty feet from the funeral home's back door, where we accepted delivery of the bodies. That also happened to be the door most of the employees used, so it was easy enough to see how Will had spotted the break-in. I could see the warehouse door was several inches ajar without even getting out of the car.

"I don't suppose I can convince you to wait in the car while I have a look?" Ben asked.

"You're kidding. Do you suddenly have magical defenses I don't know about?"

He didn't reply, just exited the car and met me around the front. When we reached the door, he said, "Let me have a look first, at least."

"Please," I replied in my most sarcastic tone. "Whoever was here is long gone by now, but I still don't want you, without even a hint of magical protection, taking the lead."

But Ben wasn't listening or didn't care. My basically defenseless boyfriend headed for the entrance as if I hadn't said a word.

I threw up a quick shield. Good thing, because he beat me there. I was inches behind him, but he still went through the doorway first.

I hugged close enough to include him in the shield I'd constructed and block a magical attack should one be waiting for us on the other side of the door, but that also made me blind to what was inside since he stood in front of the narrow gap.

Ben held out his arm behind him—as if I wouldn't slip past him in a pinch, silly man—and then looked through the gap in the doorway. He very quietly slid the door completely shut. It didn't latch, which explained the narrow gap. He had a funny look on his face that I couldn't interpret.

"What? Is it bad? Did they damage the caskets?"

"That evidence I was talking about earlier," Ben said, "something that would point to Marge having been here? Yeah, we won't be needing that." He pulled the door wide. "Say hi to Marge."

7

Marge grinned.

It was a happy dragon kind of grin. One that I interpreted to mean, "I'm really excited to see you!"

But Ben turned a paler shade of ivory than was natural for even his red-headed complexion. Probably all those sharp teeth she was flashing.

"Hi, Marge." I nudged Ben with my shoulder.

"Right, hello," he said. "Why are you hiding in my warehouse?"

Marge snorted.

"I don't think she's hiding, Ben. Especially considering those scorch marks." Marge nodded, which prompted my next question. "Weren't you worried someone else would realize you're here?"

Ben cursed, and we both turned to look at him. "Sorry. The body. Alistair's body is being delivered at ten thirty. We need to get rid of the scorch marks or..." He tipped his head at the very easily discovered elephant-sized dragon.

"Or all three of us might end up busted by emergency response when they spot Marge. That's a good point, babe. Especially with those scorch marks shouting her presence."

I was constantly amazed at his tolerance. He didn't even look angry. Worried, but not angry. I scrunched my eyes closed. Illusion was an option, but I wasn't *that* good. I could increase the growth of the surrounding and damaged vegetation, but even if I had a magically green thumb—which I didn't—it would still take hours to repair the damage Marge had made.

"Star? Hon, open your eyes."

When I did, I wasn't entirely sure I was seeing what I was seeing. Right. That sounded insane, but a dragon sticking out her long, forked tongue at the two of us wasn't any less insane than me imagining she was doing it.

"Any idea what that means in dragon speak?" Ben asked. He didn't take his eyes off the tongue that was about to drip dragon slobber on his warehouse floor.

When I shrugged, Marge snorted—which sprayed dragon slobber all over us.

"Marge!" Ben yelled.

I had to bite back a laugh. Not the hysterical kind. The honest-to-goodness hilarity-filled version. I thought Ben had no limits, but it seemed he drew the line at dragon slobber.

"So when we have kids, it's gonna be me wiping the snotty noses, isn't it?"

Ben turned to me with the remnants of his initial appalled expression. It quickly morphed to a blank look, then he grinned. "We're having kids?"

"Uh, sure, I guess. I mean, eventually. Maybe. If we—"

"Hey, it's okay." He grinned even wider. "Kids are good. I'm thinking at least three."

"What?" Kids in the abstract were good. I wanted a kid, maybe kids, at some point. But pushing out three watermelon-sized kiddos through my not-watermelon-sized hoo-ha was a disconcerting thought. "Three? Really? *Three*?"

"Sure. Maybe four." Ben laughed at the look on my face, but I wasn't sure if he was joking or just found my response entertaining. Sure, *he* could laugh. It wasn't his hoo-ha. Well, it was sort of his, but not really his. Ugh. We needed to not talk about this right now.

"Men," I muttered.

Marge snorted again. Which brought back the more pressing question of a dragon who stuck out her tongue at us and her impending discovery on Ben's property.

"Sorry, Marge," I said, "but I really don't know what you're saying."

"I'm guessing it has something to do with covering up the scorch marks," Ben said.

She reeled in that long, slobbery tongue and nodded. She even fluttered her lashes at Ben. That girl was a total flirt, even in the face of looming death-by-enraged-vampire-horde and imminent discovery by a less-than-dragon-friendly emergency response.

Ben wiped a bit of goo from his face. In its place was a distinct white mark. I stepped closer and examined the mark. "What's wrong?" Ben shot a look over my shoulder at Marge. "This stuff isn't poisonous, is it?"

Marge huffed. Even I could tell she was offended.

"Shush and lean down." I frequently forgot about our height difference, but he was easily a foot taller, and I couldn't see well enough to confirm my suspicions. Once I'd examined the mark and wiped away the rest of the small splatters, I bit my lip.

"How bad is it?" Ben asked, and again Marge huffed.

"It's about as bad as that time you got splotches of sunscreen on your pale legs. How many times do I have to tell you to spread evenly?" I patted his cheek and then turned to Marge. "Does your spit heal wounds?"

She tipped her head, neither agreeing nor disagreeing.

Ben flushed. "Burns. Her spit heals burns." When Marge nodded enthusiastically, I couldn't help a chuckle. Ben hated how easily he burned. He wore sunscreen most days, but obviously he was burned now, or Marge's spray of spit wouldn't have had any effect on him. "Laugh away. Just wait till all our kids come out redheaded and pale as sheets."

Yep, that cut my amusement short. Not that I'd mind little redheaded babies that looked just like Ben...someday. But I wasn't ready for the reality of little baby Bens *today*. We didn't even live together. Forget being married or even engaged. Kids were *so* far away.

"I'm guessing this works on vegetation?" Ben

asked Marge. When she nodded, he added, "And diluted?"

Marge grinned and looked at me.

I'd learned about dilute preparations from Camille. She was the queen of potions, and I'd picked up a few things over the last few years. "We should use distilled water to prevent complications. I think we have some in the storeroom."

Marge sighed and settled into a curled-up ball on the warehouse floor. She glanced at us and then the door.

"I think we've been dismissed," Ben said.

Since he sounded a little offended, I reminded him: "Vampire horde, Ben. Bloodthirsty vamps should be avoided at all costs. Also, overzealous fake police."

Alex, my ex, would hate being called fake police, but emergency response were hardly the real police.

Ben opened the door. "The vampire horde are hardly likely to be accompanying the body. It'll be your ex, won't it?"

"Most likely, but Alex won't be alone, and whoever accompanies him won't have any motivation to keep signs of a wanted fugitive from Cornelius. Also, I'd rather not put Alex in the position of having to choose. His first duty as the senior emergency responder is supposed to be to Cornelius."

"Supposed to be?"

"Alex is his own man, and his first duty as long as I've known him has been to his own conscience."

"Fair enough. He's really not half bad, your ex." And that was exactly the kind of man that Ben was. Not jealous, because in his mind, he had the girl, so why waste ill feelings on some guy who clearly didn't? He unlocked and then ushered me through the back door of the funeral home. "How long will it take you to mix up a dragon spit potion?"

"I'm totally calling it that. Dragon Spit Potion. It has a nice ring. Better than 'burn cure' or 'limited regeneration potion.'"

Ben didn't comment, endorse, or shoot down the name, just asked what he could do to help.

After I retrieved an appropriate glass container, I sent Ben back to collect saliva while I gathered the few other items I'd need. It wasn't quite so simple as mixing water and dragon spit. I had to make sure to preserve as much of the potency as possible. Thankfully, Camille was a masterful potion brewer, so I had a few tricks up my sleeve.

Some of those tricks took a little time to sort, so I had to get cracking. Those scorch marks needed to be gone before Alex arrived in less than two hours. And then, when I could breathe a little easier, maybe I'd ask Marge what the heck she was thinking. What was up with the scorch marks? I had to wonder if they were even intentional, because why expose herself—expose us—to discovery?

Ben returned with the beaker a quarter full and handed it to me. "How much focus does brewing this potion take?" His question was curiously bland, given the time pressure.

"Why?"

He shrugged but didn't look at me. He kept his focus on the bucket I'd sterilized to use in the potion preparation.

"Ben, spit it out. I can multitask."

"Hmm." He bit his lip, still not looking at me. "You sure about that?"

"What, already? If you don't tell me, I'll just be worried."

"Right. So, we missed a pretty big detail earlier."

After I'd dumped the saliva into the bucket, I stopped my prep and put my hands on my hips. "What in the world are you not telling me?"

Ben scrubbed his hands over his face. "I think I know why Marge ran, even though she might be innocent. She's, uh..." His face turned a light pink color I didn't see very often on him. "I saw an egg."

I shook my head, confused. "An egg?" Then understanding filtered in. "A dragon egg? Marge dropped a dragon egg in your warehouse?"

"Yeah. That happened." He looked as dismayed as I felt.

8

No pressure.

An egg-dropping dragon nesting in the warehouse, a fried body due to be delivered, and emergency response less than two hours from my doorstep.

But no pressure.

I sprinkled a few pinches of Himalayan salt into the potion with a shaking hand. A few weeks ago, I'd stashed some basic supplies at the funeral home, but nothing fancy. At least I was saved from using table salt. Iodine wasn't always a great addition to a potion.

"An egg? Why would she drop an egg here? Now? Today?" I stirred the concoction with a big metal spoon Ben had found in the tiny break room.

When it started to froth, I slowed my frantic churning to a more reasonable speed. Who knew what overstimulated dragon saliva would do? It could be flammable when agitated too strongly. "You'd think she'd find a safer place. And how can there be an egg when there aren't any boy dragons running around?"

"I knew I shouldn't have told you," Ben muttered. I shot him a peeved look, and he said, "Anything I can do to help?"

"Not that I wouldn't have mentioned the last four times you asked."

"Right. And while I don't know how dragon procreation works, chickens can lay infertile eggs. Maybe it won't hatch?"

"That's a terrible thought. Unless she's not treating it like a proper egg?"

Ben shook his head. "It's back in the corner on a pile of shredded cardboard boxes, so she's got a nest going. That's why we didn't see it at first, because it's in a dark corner and she was in front of it."

Right, so maybe it would hatch. A baby dragon. A baby Marge dragon. It would be so incredibly cute, all purply-blue and green.

"You cannot have a baby dragon as a pet."

I looked up from the potion. "Not a clue what

you're talking about. Besides, it's not like dragons are pets."

I so wanted a dragon as a pet.

"You sure? You have that look you get when you cuddle puppies."

He knew me so well. Time for a quick topic change or we'd be wandering down the kid path again.

"I just need to heat this for a few minutes and then we should be good. I don't suppose you want to test it out?" I waggled my eyebrows at him. "Even out those speckles on your face?"

"Since I know what's in that concoction, I'm gonna pass. But I can run out and test the nearest strip of charred grass."

I transferred enough of the potion to almost fill the original beaker then held it over a small Bunsen burner, swishing it gently. "You can take this batch out in a sec. If it works, we'll fill up two spray bottles and drench the marks with whatever we've got. Maybe more potion will make it work faster."

Ben glanced at the clock. "We've got about an hour and a half. You think the diluted version will take longer than the pure stuff?"

"Yeah, that's usually how it works, unfortunately. I'm giving it a little extra push of magic, but I don't know if that will speed up the process." Setting the beaker aside to cool, I added, "It's not like I've worked with dragon saliva before. I didn't even know it healed burns. It's pretty amazing stuff." Really amazing stuff. Oh, no. I cursed.

"You're thinking the horde of angry vamps will want her for more than just her blood."

"Yeah. What if they figure out what she can do? What if she can do more than just heal burns? Sucking her blood might be just the tip of the iceberg. Maybe they'll use her as some kind of horrible saliva- and blood-producing slave?" I squeezed my eyes shut. Revenge was bad enough, but add a financial motivation to the mix and things just got much more complicated.

"At least they'd have to keep her alive to do that."

"And in what condition, Ben? You know how backward the Society can be. They might let anyone who got their hands on her lock her up and use her as their own personal magical supply closet." I shuddered. Like a rat in a lab, but worse because Marge was...Marge.

I quickly filled a small test tube with the potion and handed it to Ben. "Go sprinkle this on the nearest spot and let me know if you see immediate improvement." I took a breath. "I'm gonna have a little chat with our fugitive mom."

"Good luck," Ben said before hustling out the door.

The remaining potion could marinate without ill effect, so I'd wait to see if the dilute potion I'd made worked before I cooked the rest. I had more pressing concerns: finding out how Marge's offspring would change the equation.

When I entered the warehouse, I found Marge delicately shredding box material using her teeth and claws. Her previous position curled on the floor had concealed the nest she'd made in the dark corner. Now, as she rummaged for more nesting materials, I could see the tidy little nest that she'd created for her *giant* egg. Her giant *purple* egg.

Ben had left that part out.

I approached the nest cautiously. Marge didn't seem concerned about my interest. She moved on to the stack of collapsed boxes, looking for more nesting material, so I inched closer. "It's gorgeous." I kept my hands clasped behind my back. "Such a beautiful color."

Marge smiled. But for the teeth, she'd look almost maternal.

"How long before he or she hatches?"

She tapped a long claw against the wall three times.

"Three weeks?" Please let it be three weeks. Three months would be a nightmare. No way we'd be able to keep her hidden that long. Even three weeks—

A puff of steam caught my attention. Marge shook her head and dread washed over me. "Three months?" I squeaked, the high pitch a dead giveaway for my panic.

Marge chortled softly and shook her head.

"Wait, you don't mean three *days*?" When she nodded, I said, "But didn't you just..." What did one call it? Did she lay an egg like a chicken? Or did she drop her young, like a calf? "Um, didn't you just make the egg?"

Her chest puffed with what looked like pride, and she nodded.

Amidst all the mess—Marge's flight from supposed justice, her landing unexpectedly first on my balcony and then here at the funeral home—Ben and I had missed that she was pregnant. Or maybe it hadn't been visible, either way, she'd not gotten the response from us that she should have. With a bright smile, I said, "Congratulations, Marge."

And she beamed. Just like a new mom.

"Is this your first?"

She shook her head.

"No one knew that you were, um, pregnant?" Was that what dragons were before they had an egg?

But Marge knew what I meant, because she shook her head without hesitation.

That cleared up a few questions. Not that I doubted it before, but now I knew with absolute certainty that Marge was innocent. "You would never have hurt someone right before you, um, laid an egg." She looked at me with sad eyes. The only reason I could imagine she'd put herself at risk when she was in such a delicate state would be to protect her baby—but no one knew about her condition. Dragons were notoriously secretive, so that was easy to believe. Finally, I said, "You didn't do it, did you?"

She shook her head, but it was a rhetorical question.

An explanation for those scorch marks popped into my head and if I was right, it couldn't be simpler. A dragon about to lay an egg might be having something similar to the contractions pregnant women experience. If so, I had to wonder if that might lead to some accidental fire exhalations. "I don't suppose those scorch marks had anything to with you being close to laying your egg?"

She gave me a sheepish grin and nodded.

Scorch marks explained—sort of.

The big, beautiful egg drew my gaze again. It was mottled, like an emu's egg, but instead of teal, it was a gorgeous dark purple. "Marge, your egg is the size of a Great Dane."

She fluttered her lashes and once again beamed with pride.

Maybe large egg size was a good thing in the dragon world, but given my earlier conversation with Ben about giving birth, I couldn't help wincing. "You're feeling okay?"

Her long, sinuous neck stretched closer to her egg and a dreamy look crossed her reptilian face. She nodded without taking her eyes off the egg. She was completely entranced by her little eggling.

I was bowled over by the faith she was placing in me. She was trusting me with both her and her egg's safety, and she was in a pretty darn precarious situation right now.

Huge responsibility.

Massive.

And that was one reason the loud, thudding knock scared the bejesus out of both of us.

9

Before my brain could work out the fact that bad guys didn't usually announce their presence with a knock, Alex stuck his head through the gap and hollered, "Incoming. Don't fry me."

Steam wafted slowly from Marge's nostrils and her eyes narrowed to slits. She was all sorts of scary when she wasn't flirting or glowing with maternal pride.

I stepped between her and the open door. "That's Alex. Give him a second." When her head dipped in acknowledgement of my request, I turned to the handsomely rumpled man walking through the door. "Really, Alex? 'Incoming'? You're lucky she didn't wipe out you and half of that wall."

He lifted his hands. "I come in peace. Mostly."

I could feel the heat of a pissy new momma dragon at my back. "Watch what you're saying, Alex. You don't have all the facts. And who the heck came with you?"

Please let it be someone who wouldn't rat us out. Someone who would be sympathetic to a sweet, innocent, non-vampire-frying dragon.

"Francis."

I practically crumpled in relief. "Thank goodness." Francis was good people. He'd at least listen to reason...for a few seconds.

"He's in the car with the body. The car I left parked in front of the funeral home when I saw that someone had been playing magic paint-by-numbers in your neighboring field. Thankfully, Ben caught me exiting the car, or I'd have zapped first and asked questions later when I stumbled on the giant purple-and-green fugitive in your warehouse." He rested a hip against the doorframe.

Not for a second did I mistake his casual stance for relaxation. That tall, lean body of his packed more magic than anyone else I'd met in the enhanced community. Alex was a powerful wizard, frighteningly skilled with the sword he always wore concealed on his body, and as close to a cop as the Society had.

In a word, Alex was a problem...if I couldn't convince him of Marge's innocence.

"She didn't do it."

"Uh-huh. You know this because you've autopsied the body you haven't even received? Or because you've conducted a thorough investigation in less than twenty-four hours?" His words were sharp, but he didn't shift from his position against the door. And he kept his eyes on me, not Marge.

"I have a suspect list." Which was pretty weak, so I could kinda see his point. "But I know she didn't do it, because she wouldn't have. Not now." I pointed at him. "Swear you'll keep this between us unless you have incontrovertible proof that Marge is responsible for frying Alistair."

The heat at my back ratcheted up a notch, and sweat trickled down my neck. Marge might not be happy, but we needed Alex on our side.

Alex rubbed his neck. "You know, someday, you're going to get me in serious trouble."

I smiled at him. "But you know I'm on the side of the angels, don't you?"

"Yeah, whatever. You've got my promise to keep whatever is happening here under my hat for twenty-four hours unless I stumble on proof beyond Alistair's charred corpse that Marge is responsible for his death."

No way was he agreeing to "incontrovertible" evidence, so I focused on the more important part of this deal. "Three days. I want three days."

He lost some of his devil-may-care attitude and straightened to his full height. "You've lost your mind. Three days on a case like this is an eternity. The vamps are pressuring emergency response for justice, and once they get wind that you're involved, they'll be crawling all over you and this funeral home well before three days have passed. They'll find out shortly that you're doing the autopsy. Clarice is pissed that she was passed over on this job and is already moaning to anyone who will listen."

Clarice, Cornelius's resident witch resource for magical autopsies, could stuff it. I didn't know her well, but she wasn't the brightest if she was vocal in her complaints. Discretion was almost as valued as skill or power in the enhanced world. I'd deal with her later if it became a problem.

"I guess the vamp horde and Clarice are my problem, but I want those three days."

Alex shook his head. "You're sure she's worth it?"

Steam drifted around me, but I ignored it and

waited for him to decide if he'd trust me.

Finally, he let his gaze drift over my shoulder to Marge. "I'll agree to the three days, but only if you'll call when you need help. And you know you will at some point, so don't even try to deny it."

"Done," I said quickly, before he could change his mind. "And the reason I know Marge wouldn't do this?" I looked over my shoulder to find Marge standing protectively in front of her nest. I couldn't even see that it was a nest, so well had she blocked the view. Turning back to Alex, I said, "Marge is gonna be a momma."

Alex whistled. For the first time, he looked like he might believe me. "Congratulations, Marge." He directed the comment over my shoulder and even accompanied it with what passed for a smile. A quirk around the edges of his lips and a little crinkle at the corner of his eyes. That was legit, warm emotion coming from him. Who knew Alex was a softy for babies?

He motioned for me to follow him outside the warehouse. Once he'd closed the door behind us, he said, "You have got to make sure that no one gets their hands on that egg. With some magical persuasion, that baby might imprint on someone not its momma."

"And that would be bad?"

"Very bad. Flying magical weapon bad." Alex sighed. "How did your boyfriend's funeral home end up as the nesting place of one the last dragons in the US?" He closed his eyes and shook his head. When he opened them, he looked both baffled and annoyed. "How did she even manage to get the egg fertilized?"

I shrugged. "Any way that someone would know she's here?"

"I don't think so. Clean up the massive magical residue that's covering your field, on the off chance anyone makes their way out here and starts asking questions about it. And bury Alistair's body as quickly as you can. I'll make sure Francis keeps his mouth shut."

"Right." I'd have to trust that Alex could do that. I liked Francis, but he was still an emergency responder and ultimately under Cornelius's leadership.

"It's fine, Star. I kept him in the car for a reason. He knows something's going on, but he doesn't know it's related to Marge. And he owes me."

I raised my eyebrows.

"He owes me big. He'll keep quiet. You need to start on that body and get it gone." He waved in the general direction of the funeral home, as if ushering me would make me move faster.

First I checked in with Marge and saw she'd settled down into her nest, then I headed to the funeral home back door. "How exactly do you expect me to hide a bunch of magic?"

Ben must have used that first potion batch I'd cooked up and treated all of the scorch marks. No clue how he'd made that single beaker stretch far enough, unless Marge's magic and my own were particularly simpatico. That happened sometimes, where the combined whole was significantly more powerful than its constituent parts.

"If you don't have the ability to hide it, then you need to give anyone who sees it a reason for its presence."

"Right." I stopped just shy of the door and turned to look at the field. Using a touch of magical sight, I examined the field—and found it glowing with an abundance of magic. Too much magic. Way too much. "Holy seashells. How did that happen?"

"You're saying it's not yours?"

"Well, mine and Marge's. But..." I glanced back at the field. "Wow."

Simpatico was an understatement. More like our magic got together and made a love child. Oops.

Alex shook his head. "You're a mess. Sort your magic. Sort your dragon. Sort it all before you have a bunch of pissed-off vamps banging on your door and no one around to make sure they don't drain you dry."

"Nice, Alex. Like I can't handle some pissy vamps." I probably could handle some pissy vamps. Depending on *how* pissy they were.

He didn't comment, just stared.

"I won't forget that I promised to call if I need help."

He kept staring.

"And I'll do my best not to need help."

He sighed. "Good enough for now. I wish you'd be more careful."

Of course he did. Alex was a worrier with a deeply ingrained hero complex. He needed to solve everyone's problems, but he wasn't going to solve mine...if I could help it.

As I watched him return to the car carting around Alistair's charred remains, I really hoped I could manage this mess on my own.

If I did need him and he wasn't there to save the day because I'd chased him off, it wouldn't be just me who suffered. Ben, Marge, and her little eggling would, as well.

10

"He's certainly crunchy." Ben wasn't nearly as bothered by Alistair's hunched and blackened form as I was.

"You see a lot of these?" In the months I'd been at the funeral home, I'd yet to see anything quite like this. When Ben and Francis brought the body in, they'd warned us to be careful handling it. A small bit of *something* had already fallen off due to the brittle condition of the body. I made Ben pick that up.

"No, of course not. Why do you ask?" He didn't even look up from his examination.

"Because your stomach seems to be handling this really well. The smell doesn't bother you?"

He pulled a small tub of menthol rub out of his cargo shorts pocket and offered it to me.

"No thanks. I already tried that. Now I'm getting mixtures of crispy critter and liniment. Not really a good combo." When Ben's eyes widened, I realized how inappropriate my comment had been. "Uh, sorry."

"People deal with stressful situations in different ways. I, of all people, know that. But maybe go ahead and get rolling. The sooner you're done, the sooner he's gone." Ben frowned. "This is like the other vamp clients, right? No preservation, plain box, burial in a Society plot?"

Ben had handled a few newbie vamp burials. In the vamp world, the younger you were, the more likely you were to die. Age conveyed greater power, more knowledge, and better connections.

"Yeah. No one said differently. And Cornelius said he was done with the body insofar as any investigation." I peered at the corpse, then looked with my magical sight. Flames. I could still see flames. And that made me think of burning. More accurately, burning bodies, and—

"Star!" Ben pulled me away. "Hey. Watch it. You turned pale all of a sudden." Standing between me and the body, he asked, "What did you see?"

"Fire."

Ben groaned. "Like the flames you saw when you had a look at Marge's scorch marks?"

"Oh, no." I wasn't sure why I didn't make that connection immediately. Maybe it was the smell or maybe the pressure. Marge and the eggling were counting on me. I leaned to the side and got another look with my sight wide open. Flames, like before but not exactly. "No, definitely not the same. There are flames, but they're a different color. These are brilliant red, not orange."

"Doesn't flame color reflect the heat or the fuel? I doubt those scorch marks outside were made by as hot a flame as what Alistair encountered, whatever the source or sources of the fire."

"Different fuel might burn at different temperatures and produce different colors." I grinned at him. "But that's not how magic works, sweetie."

My grin must have been catching, because he flashed one back at me. "Marge didn't fry this guy, did she?"

I kissed him, and for just a second, there was nothing in the room but us. Only Ben could make me forget everything. After a few seconds, I stepped away and said, "I don't know how you do it, but you can be romantic and make me feel romantic in just about any setting." I very determinedly did *not* look at the other occupant of the room. "And yes, we now have proof that Marge's flame didn't do this."

"As simple as that? That witch Clarice really is terrible."

"Eh, not really. Well, maybe she is, but this wasn't her fault. Without evidence of Marge's magic—in our case, the scorched field—there's no baseline for comparison. There *is* clear evidence that magic caused the burns, just not Marge's magic. I'll have to poke around to see what or who else has magical fire, but I'm guessing it's not a common talent, otherwise Marge wouldn't be in the fix she's in."

"I meant to ask before, couldn't someone whip up a fire potion?" Ben asked. "That would make the pool of suspects a lot bigger." After spending a little time with Camille, he was convinced any magical mountain could be conquered with the right spell or potion.

Camille was the best potions witch in Austin by far, so his opinion was well founded. Heck, she'd baked up a realistic dead body replica.

"*I* can't, though I'm sure Camille can." I shot him a smile. "But don't worry. This wasn't potion magic. That much even Clarice would have seen. I'm thinking we're looking at a creature—maybe another dragon?—because I don't know of any person with that kind of talent locally."

"Another dragon...as in Marge's baby daddy?"

"Oh, wow. I hope not." It looked like I needed to have another chat with Marge. How did one ask an elephant-sized, fire-breathing creature with fangs and claws the size of Ben's hands if her romantic interest might possibly have roasted our victim?

Marge was pretty much a pussycat. Pretty much. But... "Hey, Ben, maybe we save that conversation for after we've disposed of the corpse and have ticked a few suspects off our interview list."

He cocked an eyebrow. "So, about that disposal —are you going to finish your autopsy?"

What with all of the distraction of the discovery I'd made about the flame signature not matching Marge's, I'd unknowingly been acclimating to the odor. I was ready to finish up.

About five minutes into my head-to-toe inspection, Ben's mobile phone rang. "Camille." He handed it to me.

Thank goodness this autopsy was hands-off.

"Hey, Camille. What's up?"

"Suze came through. I've got you set up to see Lisette in an hour."

"An hour!" I pressed my lips together, but too late. I couldn't take that screech of distress back.

Ben's hand landed on my shoulder, calming me a little. He rubbed my back and said, "I've got the body. We need to stash it, in case they need some kind of proof, but I have an idea about that. You make the meeting, and I'll handle it."

Camille's voice pulled my attention back to the phone. "Listen to your boyfriend. If you found something that points to another suspect, then you should stash it. Preferably not on the property."

I looked at Ben, and he nodded that he'd heard her.

"All right," I agreed. Poor Ben. He was not equipped for this, but I couldn't be late and we couldn't just leave the corpse hanging out in the prep room or the cooler. I sighed. "Where's this meeting?"

11

B en could handle hiding a charred body.
Sure he could.
No problem.

And if he couldn't, it didn't matter. Evidence preservation couldn't be my focus at the moment. Not when I had bigger—or at least more immediate —troubles.

Lisette arranged to meet me at a quiet café in south Austin. They were known for their pancakes. I loved pancakes. Too bad I was on the verge of ralphing and wouldn't be able to enjoy them. Actually, vamps couldn't eat solids, so the good news was I wouldn't have to watch Lisette devour a divine breakfast while I tried not to upchuck.

Vamps generally made me a little nervous,

because I didn't have a ton of experience with them. Also, they were creepy and gross. Bloodsucking could do that to one's image.

But it was more the time factor that was stressing me out. The funeral home wasn't in Austin. I was a good twenty-minute drive from the café, and I needed to get there early to set up some protections. We could hardly have a conversation about vampires, witches, magic, and dead people in the middle of a café without raising a few eyebrows. Sure, it was south Austin, but blood, gore, death, and magic were a little much even for the "keep Austin weird" crowd.

I pulled into the café's parking lot about thirty minutes before the designated meet time and still hadn't beaten Lisette here. Unless the sparkling Mercedes convertible with the "I 🖤 Dracula" sticker and the plastic fangs swinging from the rearview mirror belonged to some other patron.

Apparently Lisette had a sense of humor. I didn't think vamps laughed—ever.

My stomach swirled. Now I had to throw around some privacy shields like it was no big thing, when constructing one required all of my concentration.

That might have explained my grumpy mood when I entered the café. Or it was the smell of complete perfection that assaulted my nose as I entered, combined with the certainty my stomach couldn't handle the tasty awesomeness.

Or maybe it was the lurking dragon in my boyfriend's warehouse. The one whose life—and that of her unhatched eggling—was resting on my shoulders. Yeah, that was likely the biggest part.

Whatever the cause, I walked in with my grumpy pants on.

Imagine my surprise when Lisette—vampy, blood-drinking, take-no-prisoners Lisette—greeted me with a smile.

It wasn't even twitchy or showing fang.

And then she reached out her hand like a friendly human would, all genuine warmth and southern charm. Was there a full moon?

I shook her hand even though it wasn't a common greeting in the enhanced community, then joined her at the table she indicated. The table she'd already managed to enclose in a cone of magical privacy. It looked like Lisette had her own witchy resources. My bet was on a personal charm she could activate when needed. That had to be it, because there certainly wasn't a witch hidden away on the premises.

"Thank you for meeting me." She had a slight accent, perhaps French, given her name.

Camille had mentioned that Odette, Alistair's most recent love interest, had fallen into the arm-candy arena. Looking at the curvy, petite brunette in front of me, I had to guess that Alistair liked his ladies lovely.

"Ah, I think that's my line?" Hadn't we reached out to her? Via Suze, the trusty PA, my tired brain replied. And now I was having conversations in my head.

I needed some more sleep. Nah. I needed to solve this mystery and reduce my stress.

"Well, yes, you did schedule the meeting, but I would have contacted you once I realized you were investigating Alistair's death." She leaned forward, her chocolate-brown eyes wide. "It's all been such a shock. I can't believe anyone would do this to Alistair." But then her eyes narrowed and a glint of red sparked in their depths. That was more like the vamps I'd come to know and dislike. "I find it very difficult to believe a simpleminded dragon got the drop on Alistair. You have to find the vamp who fried him."

Whoa. So not everyone thought Marge was guilty? This put a new spin on things. Unless this was typical vamp trickery and a preemptive strike. Maybe I was sitting across from Alistair's murderer.

As I contemplated her words, she flagged down our waitress and ordered a hot apple cider and two mimosas.

"You look like you need a little pick-me-up." Lisette arched a perfectly plucked eyebrow and waited for me to deny it.

I wanted to say, "No, I just look this frazzled and frumpy all the time," but I refrained. I was technically still a student, so jeans and a hoody weren't *that* out of place. Also, I'd been rolled rather precipitously out of bed this morning and rushed out the door to attend to an emergency.

Speaking of that emergency... "Everyone seems convinced that Marge is the responsible party."

Lisette waved a dismissive hand. "Please. Clarice is hardly the most competent choice to handle this matter. I don't trust her conclusion, especially since she reached it so quickly. Clarice doesn't work quickly. But there is also the matter of Cornelius. Cleary he has no faith in her results or you wouldn't have been given an opportunity to examine the body."

Our waitress appeared, entering the protected space between Lisette and me as she leaned in to deliver our drinks. Once she'd moved outside Lisette's protected circle and could no longer hear us, Lisette continued, "It's lazy investigating. Any creature that possesses magical fire could have done the damage. Without a sample of the dragon's flame, there's no way that Clarice could definitively say it was dragon fire that did the damage, let alone a particular dragon's fire."

The room warmed by about five degrees. Before she noticed the guilty flush splashed across my face, I said, "And why do you care?"

There. My bold question would hopefully distract her, or she'd think asking such a direct question had flustered me. Which it had. Now the room felt like an oven.

She considered me with her head tipped slightly at an angle, and I saw that flash of red deep in her eyes again. It was called bleeding red. When vamps lost control of their emotions or when they fed, so I heard, their eyes glowed a brilliant red. These brief glimpses were the only time I'd seen the effect up close and personal.

"I always thought it would be me that killed him." The words were quiet, barely a whisper.

"You hated him for leaving you?" I couldn't believe the question popped out of my mouth.

But she just smiled. Not even a glimpse of fang. "No, I loved him. In a way that may be foreign to you, but it's love as I know it."

If I didn't know better, I'd say she was putting the whammy on me, because I believed her. I had protections in place to avoid mental manipulation. I fingered the thin bracelet I wore. It was still packed full of magical juice, which meant I was still protected.

And yet—I believed her.

She smiled again. "And if I'd killed him, the world would know. I'd have ripped his throat out and watched him bleed to death." There was an amused twinkle in her eyes as she watched my reaction.

I didn't think she was pulling my leg.

She waited as I inspected her expression, and the amusement didn't waiver.

Nope. She wasn't kidding. She would have ripped his throat out, killed him with all the passion she held in her heart. What was left of her heart.

What she wouldn't have done was gone to elaborate lengths to hide her crime. No charred body. No false accusation of death by dragon.

"You didn't do it." This time, it wasn't a slip of the tongue. I didn't believe that she had.

"I did not." A small wrinkle formed between her eyes. "It's difficult to believe anyone did. He was cautious."

"Okay, so who was more devious than Alistair?" At her contemptuous look, I added, "Or was within his circle of trust and may have caught him unawares?"

She laughed.

It was a rusty sound, as if laughter was foreign to her. I was sure it was, all signs of a possible lurking sense of humor aside.

"What about the three Ms?" I asked, cutting off the last of her chuckles.

"The three Ms? Ah, Alistair's entourage. They couldn't harm him."

"But they had the greatest access, and—"

"No. You misunderstand. It's not that they wouldn't, but that they are incapable. The idiots are bound by a blood contract to do him no harm."

"You're certain?" Because this not only confirmed the rumor Camille had heard, but it made it almost impossible for one of them to harm Alistair.

"Oh, yes. Complete chuckleheads, those three. Why anyone would make such a contract with Alistair, I don't know." My confusion must have shown, because she rolled her eyes and said, "Just because I loved the egocentric jerk doesn't mean I was blind to his faults or that I trusted him."

What an interesting life to live. Not one I'd want, but certainly interesting. I'd stick with my much-less-complicated love life, thank you very much.

I didn't need complicated or difficult or messy. I just needed Ben. And if things went the direction of complicated or difficult or messy at some point, we'd deal with it because we loved each other. But none of those things were in themselves attractive to me. I suspected that was part of Alistair's charm for Lisette.

"What about Odette?"

Lisette shrugged. "Perhaps, but doubtful."

"You don't seem...bothered by her existence." That was about as subtly as I could word it. Lisette was the discarded woman, one who still carried a torch for her former lover. Odette was the more current mistress of the dead man. How could Alistair inspire passion in the woman sitting so serenely across the table from me, and yet mention of her replacement didn't elicit any observable emotion?

"I'm not particularly bothered. Her relationship with Alistair was separate from my own." She arched that fine eyebrow again. "Have you been listening to rumors, little witch? Alistair and I were still very much involved."

"But you're no longer business partners."

A humorless bark of laughter erupted from her mouth. "By my choice. Because Alistair was an abysmal businessman. He only skated by on his connections. Fresh money always coming in to shore up his terrible financial decisions. The man was a disaster in business."

If that was case, then who better to resent him and wish him dead than his closest business partner? "Then Bob Smith must have motive."

"Darling, who *have* you been talking to? Bob Smith is worth a fortune. Not a meager, human-sized fortune. A vampire-sized fortune. Bob kept Alistair around for his connections, certainly not for his business acumen. In fact, you'll find that the oh-so-clever Bob didn't let Alistair anywhere near the decision-making in their joint ventures."

"But then who wanted Alistair dead?" My suspect list had just been shredded. I'd have to follow up, naturally, but if what she was saying was true, who had a motive to kill Alistair?

She leveled me with a cold stare. "I haven't a clue. And that, little witch, is why we're meeting today."

Our mimosas, which had been happily fizzing away as we spoke, now looked even more absurdly merry.

If Lisette wasn't completely off base, I hadn't a single suspect.

She lifted her mimosa and said, "To finding Alistair's killer."

Except when I raised my glass in response, it didn't feel like a toast. It felt like a threat.

12

As I contemplated how I was going to corroborate—or disprove—the information I'd received from Lisette, I tried to keep the hint of panic edging ever nearer at bay. Having a meltdown while driving my boyfriend's car down the freeway wasn't a good plan.

Besides, Lisette was likely wrong and had overlooked some motivation or desire to do Alistair harm.

But what if she was right? What if her information was good? Then I had *no* suspects.

Could one of the three Ms break a blood contract? No way. If those binding contracts existed, then they were out. I had to agree with Lisette. It seemed foolish of them to have entered a contract under such terms, but if they had, they were off my list.

The three Ms were all relatively new vampires, so perhaps they hadn't understood the full ramifications of entering into such a contract, that they would be defenseless against Alistair. Or Alistair had more star power than I'd guessed. Or more something: money, access to easy blood—that was a pleasant thought— or maybe access to all his vaunted connections.

My heart fluttered as panicky feelings pushed at me again. I happened to catch a glimpse of the speedometer in my peripheral vision and about gave myself a heart attack. I slowed down to a more reasonable five miles over the speed limit, considered my not-excellent state of mind, and slowed another five miles.

Odette. She was still a prospect. Lisette might have dismissed Alistair's other, newer mistress out of hand, but she didn't say why, and I'd been too distracted to grill her.

As for the Bob Smith situation, I should be able to easily confirm with Cornelius. Hmm. Perhaps Alex. Alex would know, and he was easier to talk to.

I groaned. I hated asking him for help. But I needed to use what resources I had because it was already midday, and Marge's eggling was hatching day after tomorrow.

Alex might also know who in the area would be the most informed about magical critters. Maybe a Djinn. They had a special relationship with their own animal partners, as Marge had with her Djinn before she'd passed, but they were also more closely connected to the nonverbal members of the enhanced community. They were the magical realm equivalent of the crazy cat and dog lovers in the mundane world.

If there was a Djinn in Austin, I'd bet he or she knew what kind of animal would be capable of inflicting the damage done to Alistair.

The edges of panic receded finally.

I had a plan. Check out Bob Smith's financial situation with Alex, set up an interview with Odette, and scope out local magical critters, possibly via a local Djinn, if there was one.

The three Ms were basically off the list at this point. They'd never been good candidates to begin with, more proximity suspects than anything else.

I pulled into the funeral home driveway with a sigh of relief. A plan. I had a plan. It would all be fine. Marge's eggling would hatch safely. We'd keep the vampire horde away. Ben and I would find the killer.

Or Ben, *Alex*, and I would, because Alex's truck was parked in the parking lot.

Just spiffy.

The most pressing question just became: which boyfriend was I going to strangle?

The current one for calling in my ex without asking? Never mind that I'd planned to ask for Alex's help myself. That was completely beside the point.

Or my ex for showing up uninvited, because his hero complex wouldn't let the little witch handle her own magical mess?

As I pulled into Ben's spot, they both turned with varying looks of guilt plastered on their faces.

The moment I opened the door, Ben said, "I called him. Basically."

"Basically?" I looked at Alex, but, freakishly, he deferred to Ben.

"I called Camille because I figured if anyone could hide a corpse in plain sight, she could." He gave me a sheepish smile.

"So the plan you had in mind when I left for my appointment was to keep Alistair's body here, but to use some kind of magic to shield him." I mean, it wasn't a *terrible* plan, but that wouldn't have held up to close scrutiny.

"Yeah, but Camille sent Alex to fetch it. She said she had a better spot, and that he owed her big."

Alex lifted his hand. "I do owe her a favor, one she's cashing in, so technically I'm not interfering with your investigation."

I scratched my neck. "About that." He waited with a neutral expression, but I could swear he reeked of smug satisfaction. "Lisette punched a huge hole in my suspect list, so I had a few questions for you."

"How huge?" Ben asked. He knew exactly how long the thing had been to begin with.

"Huge enough to leave me with no suspects, if her information was good."

Alex whistled, then said, "Although, really, I don't know who would want him dead. He was powerfully connected, but not a real player in the business scene. And his women were always surprisingly loyal to him, even after he dumped them. He was an enigma."

"Oh, Lisette claims they were still an item. Her dumped status was a false rumor, per her. But really, why are they so enamored? He was creepy."

Alex just shook his head.

"And what's with him not being a player in the business scene?" Ben asked. "I thought he was involved in all sorts of partnerships, with Odette and also Bob Smith."

"Partnership is a strong word. His name was attached to a number of ventures, but he only had small financial stakes in them. He was a bad business decision waiting to happen." Alex scratched his jaw. "He had skills. He could be incredibly persuasive, and he certainly knew how to manipulate, but that's not where his interest lay. Everyone in the community has been burned by him, so within the last few decades, he hasn't had a real say in the financial side of any business, not in the way he'd have liked."

All of which confirmed what Lisette told me.

"Did he lose anyone a lot of money?" Money always seemed like a great motive to me. A lot of decisions in the witch world were made based on cash.

"Not in a long time." And I knew Alex's "long time" trumped mine, so a really long time. Alex continued, "He simply didn't have the access to lose anyone large sums. His reputation precluded that kind of involvement. I'm surprised Camille wasn't aware."

"Yeah, she might be more distanced from the day-to-day workings of the non-witch world than either of us realized." Live and learn. Next time, I'd go to Alex or even Cornelius for the latest non-witchy gossip.

"If your suspect list has imploded, then I don't know what to tell you. I don't know anyone off the top of my head who would want him dead."

"You're not the first to say that." And then the alarm bells started to ding. Alex wasn't the first, or even the second, to say that. Was Alistair leading some kind of double life? Well, beyond what every secretive, bloodsucking fiend led, because all vamps were living a double life by default.

Ben bumped my shoulder with his. "What are you thinking?"

"I'm thinking Alex isn't the first to comment that no one would have wanted to kill Alistair, and that's just weird. The guy was a vampire. Vampires are generally disliked and more violent than most. And I was under the impression that Alistair, despite his lack of financial savvy, was a powerful figure in the community."

"More a figurehead than a powerful figure," Alex said.

I threw my hands up in frustration. "Someone

wanted the guy dead. We have a corpse that proves it."

And then it hit me. We had *a* corpse. But was it *Alistair's* corpse?

"Who did the identification of the body?"

Alex's gaze narrowed with suspicion. "The three Ms, as you've nicknamed them. Not the brightest of individuals. You think Alistair's alive."

"That sneaky, nasty bastard." My blood was boiling, because poor Marge was caught up in the middle of this entire mess. Her life and that of her eggling were in danger, quite possibly over some stupid vampire politics.

Alex tipped his head. "You expected better from a vampire?" But contrary to his neutral tone, he was looking pretty ticked off.

Ben looked about as angry as I was feeling. "How do we prove it? If we can't prove it, then this guy's women and his influential connections will be demanding Marge's blood."

I was pretty sure Lisette wouldn't be, because she'd flat-out said she didn't think Marge had done it, but what about the others? Would they be as discriminating?

"We need the fire starter," I said. "If we can find what started the magical fire that charred the corpse to a crisp, maybe we'll find a connection to Alistair. And if we don't, at least we'll have evidence that Marge isn't responsible."

"You work on that." With a grim look, Alex said, "I'm going hunting."

I almost felt sorry for Alistair if Alex caught him. No. No, I didn't. Not even a little.

13

————

I nudged Alex to consider his priorities, because I'd never had much success in telling him what to do.

I suggested that he should perhaps deliver the corpse—a now even more vital piece of evidence—to its new hiding spot before going off on a quest to find the possibly not-so-dead Alistair.

He reluctantly agreed.

He also gave me the name of a source. He called him a magical creatures dealer, and handed me a wad of cash to be used as a bribe. This source was definitely no Djinn.

While he and Ben once again shifted the crumbly bits of the unnamed man, Ben asked, "Do we even know if this guy is a vampire? Could you tell that when you examined him?"

"Yes, I could tell, and yes, he is. There was no magic residue or any indication of age or power, so nothing that would help identify him in that regard."

Alex brushed his hands together after getting Mr. X stashed in the back of his truck. "You didn't get any sense of remnant power?"

I shook my head. "Is that unusual?" It's not like I routinely did autopsies, and Camille was hardly an expert, but I'd think I'd know if dead people usually left magical signatures.

I knew from personal experience that if the remains of a golem weren't properly handled, at least one with defaced creation tattoos, there could be some energy drain of nearby magical persons, but that was a very specific scenario. Of all the dead vamps I'd encountered since working at the funeral home, none of them had any kind of residual energy attached.

"I'd think an older vamp would take some time to lose all of his magic."

"Oh. You know, I've only ever helped with young vamps." I looked over my shoulder at the funeral home sign. "Since Ben got the contract for enhanced funeral services, we've had a handful. Maybe this vampire isn't very old."

Alex nodded, but his mind was already miles away. Likely strategizing how he'd find Alistair. Not a good plan to try and pull a fast one on emergency response. The Society didn't care about much, as a rule, except reveal scandals. *We must remain hidden* was kind of the unofficial motto of the Society. But Alex had a strong sense of justice, and in the years I'd known him, he was having an increasingly difficult time caging that beast, the Society's rules be damned.

"Go get him, Alex," I said, with a fond smile. "Just try not to get yourself drained. Oh, and hide the body first."

He nodded, a grim look on his face. I really wasn't into the dark and broody types, so how had I ever ended up with him?

"How were you guys a couple?" Ben asked as Alex's truck retreated down the drive. "I mean, outside of the fact that he's incredibly good looking and has more magic than any five normal wizards."

"Outside of that, I'm not really sure." I pulled Ben's head down and planted a kiss on him. I really did adore this man.

There was a noticeable lack of groping

happening while we kissed, and once I noticed, I realized why and stepped quickly away.

Lifting his hands, Ben said, "I'll just go wash up, and then we can hit the pet shop."

Yep, we were headed to a pet shop, because that was a logical front for an illicit magical creatures dealer. Actually, I shouldn't make fun. It kind of *was* a great front.

Twenty-five minutes later, Ben and I were parked in front of what looked like a normal, mundane pet shop. Puppies in one window, kittens in the other, and kids with their moms wandering by to window shop. There was a shoe store next door, so the pet store probably got decent foot traffic.

"Let's do this." I tugged Ben's hand, pulling him behind me as I approached the store.

"No plan?"

I stuttered to a stop. "We want a salamander?"

"And when they say they don't sell them? Or try to sell us the regular variety?"

I grinned at him. "Then we ask for the special kind. And I'll do a little sweep of the place with my sight to see if there are any special creatures in the store, so I should have a better idea of what's going on once we're inside."

Ben sighed. "Okay. But somehow I doubt it'll be that easy."

When we walked in, I encountered the first surprise. There wasn't an ounce of magic in the place. No shields that might be hiding magical critters. No wards to alert to the presence of enhanced visitors entering the building. No flashy security. No magical bells or whistles at all. Certainly no magical beasts.

Ben caught my eye, and I shook my head.

"How can I help you on this fabulous day?" a teenager asked us, her bored tone in direct conflict with her words. She held an open book in her hand and didn't bother to set it down or even mark her place.

This was the magical creatures dealer I was supposed to bribe? He was a she, and she couldn't be more than seventeen or eighteen.

Ben recovered faster than me. "We're here to look at your salamanders."

"Back wall. Look all you like." Before she'd finished speaking, she'd already turned her attention back to her book. She dropped down onto the stool situated in front of the register, completely ignoring us.

I tipped my head, indicating the back of the store. Might as well check it out, just in case my scan had missed something—though I didn't think it had.

The aisles were crowded with pet supplies, but tidy. When we reached the back wall, we found salamanders. No special, fire-breathing varieties that I could see, but at least four different kinds of normal, everyday salamanders.

They all looked shiny and reptilian.

And that was it.

Ben nudged me back toward the front of the store. "Your turn this time."

This time, the girl didn't even look up from her book, and, in the same bored tone, said, "Have a good day."

"We're still looking." I tried to make eye contact, but she wouldn't look up. "My boyfriend and I are trying to find a special kind of salamander."

The girl—Natalie, according to her name tag—huffed out a heavy breath and then set her book down. "Look, we've already sold that one, but I think you know that. There aren't any rules against selling fire salamanders unless we sell to mundanes. So get lost, cop."

She was looking at me when she said "cop." Not

that either Ben or I remotely looked like law enforcement. I was still in my jeans and hoody, and Ben looked like... I gave him a quick up-down assessment. In his cargo shorts and polo, he looked more like an after-hours accountant than an off-duty cop.

With another huff of annoyance, Natalie pointed with two fingers, first at her own eyes, then mine. "I see you, witch."

"Ah." Some non-magical people could see magic. It wasn't all that common, but it existed. It looked like Natalie was one of the few. Not only was she a member of that group, but it looked like she'd found a way to earn a buck on the fringes of the enhanced community using her special skill. She just seemed awfully young to be trading in near-black-market goods. "This is your store?"

She shook her head, her face clouded with disbelief. "Do I look old enough to own a store? You're, like, the worst cop ever."

"I'm not a cop. Or even emergency response." I wasn't sure why I was in such a snit, but it bothered me to be falsely labeled.

Natalie crossed her arms. "No? Then why do you care?"

I drew a breath to say—I wasn't sure what, because Ben's hand fell lightly on my back, reminding me that I was the adult (sort of) here. I could be adultlike...with a little help from Ben. In a pretty darn calm tone of voice, I said, "I think someone used the fire salamander to kill a vampire and frame someone else."

She gasped. "Not Marge?"

How did we get from fire salamanders to Marge in less than two seconds?

For the first time, Natalie looked properly engaged with the conversation. "It has to be Marge. Dragon and salamander fire burn the hottest. Marge wouldn't hurt anyone. Well, not anyone human." Her nose wrinkled. "She just roasts squirrels and things like that."

"And a fire salamander would hurt someone?" Ben asked.

"Yeah. I mean, maybe not on purpose. They're not like dragons." She grimaced. "They're not all that smart, you know? They're more like the ones at the back of the store than you'd think."

"But someone could use a fire salamander to hurt another person." If that was true, then tying Alistair to the purchase of one would be a vital link. Assuming we weren't all off our game and Alistair really was still alive.

"Sure." She looked between Ben and me. "But I

don't know who that would be. Really. I didn't sell it. That's my dad's thing. I just take care of the contraband—that's what Dad calls the magical animals—and make sure they're treated right while we have them."

"We need to speak with your father." Ben still hadn't removed his hand from my back, and I was glad that one of us was staying completely calm.

"Uh, good luck. He must have made a mint on that salamander, because he left town right after he sold it." She looked down at her book with longing, and then muttered, "Probably gambling in Vegas. Won't be back for weeks."

"What about sales records?" I asked.

"Really, lady?" All of Natalie's teenage attitude came rushing back. "Sales records for the magical creatures we sell? The ones that are mostly legal to sell, sort of, but not really. Right, let me run and go get those." She snorted. "Please."

Ben ran his hand up and down my back—not like I was going to lose it, but I still appreciated the sentiment. Very quietly and politely, he asked, "Do you know when the sale happened?"

"Two days ago. Lucifer wasn't in his cage when I got back from class." She blushed. "Um, Lucifer is what I called him."

And that fit our timeline just right. We needed to find Lucifer to verify it was his flame that crisped the corpse and not Marge's.

Ben and I exchanged a glance. He looked as stumped as I did. Not only could we not tie Alistair to Lucifer's purchase, but our one witness was AWOL in Vegas, and that was assuming he was still alive.

"If there's anything you can think of," I said, "anything to indicate who purchased Lucifer, that information would be helpful in defending Marge."

"Or if you know of a way that we might find Lucifer..." Ben didn't voice the obvious: if the tiny critter was still even alive.

Natalie must have seen something on Ben's face that clued her in to his thoughts, because her eyes widened. "Oh, you know they're really hard to kill, right? Lucy's likely running around somewhere. I mean, no telling where, but somewhere. It took Dad ages to trap one. They're tricky little guys to find."

So Alistair could have used the creature, turned him loose, and been relatively certain no one would stumble upon it for weeks, maybe months or longer. Just spiffy.

"Right. Thanks for your help," Ben said.

"Wait!" Natalie called. "No one would really

believe that Marge did it, right? She's not going to be in trouble?" She must have read the worry on our faces, because her face squished up like she was trying not to cry. Poor kid. "Why would Marge hurt anyone? She wouldn't do that. She's really sweet."

I didn't want to say it aloud, but that didn't always matter with the Society. When the available evidence pointed one way, a victim had friends demanding blood, and when the only suspect couldn't easily defend herself, well, that wasn't a good situation for Marge.

"How do you know her?" Ben asked.

"Um, I'm not supposed to say." She looked at both of us, squinted as if she could see through us, then sighed. "You're helping her, so I don't see the harm. Dad played 'matchmaker' for her. It's not like there are a bunch of dragons cruising around in the States."

Some sleazy black-market dealer with a possible gambling problem knew about Marge's eggling. That could not be good.

"Oh, don't worry." Natalie smiled. "Marge is a really good negotiator. Dad's got a monthly supply of saliva and venom coming in for at least a few months, so he'll be quiet that long."

Venom? Dragons had venom? That was a scary thought.

"Well, that's good news," Ben said, holding her gaze. "Because it's a really bad idea for anyone to know about Marge's particular condition, especially right now."

She blinked. "I won't say anything. I really liked her. Oh, hey, I just thought of something that might help. Fire salamanders need special food if you want them to spark up a flame."

Ben and I both perked up.

"Like what?" I asked, glancing around the small shop.

She gave us both a put-upon look. "Special, meaning nothing you're going to get here. It's not like I wanted Lucy sparking and setting the place on fire while he was here."

I stared back at her, because where in the world would one purchase feed for a magical salamander?

She sighed. "Really? No ideas? You guys aren't very good at this black-market-investigating stuff. Try a witch. You know, the place you'd go to get most hard-to-find stuff?"

"Right." I ignored the teenage attitude, because she wanted to help Marge and was trying to do the right thing, if a little rudely. "We'll do that."

And I didn't even have to call Camille for this one. I knew just who to ask about shady, magical creature foodstuffs.

14

"**T**ime to call CeeCee and Bernard," I said once we were safely stashed inside Ben's car.

Ben nodded. "Your friends from the Halloween party. I liked them." He pulled out of the parking lot. "Where am I headed?"

"A cute little vintage store in south Austin. That's the front for their new business."

"Wow, that was fast."

I couldn't help a laugh, because in that same time Ben and I had become pretty serious. I mean, we'd been talking about kids without either of us having a coronary. In my book, that was serious.

"What?" he said, looking all cutely confused. "Didn't they get together just before the party? And now they have a business together? The paperwork for a partnership alone, and then finding the space —they must have hustled."

"And here I was thinking that you meant the two of them going into business together was fast."

He shrugged. "Nah. They seemed solid. But, ah, why are we headed there? I thought Bernard was a spells specialist? And CeeCee specialized in potions, right?"

"Bernard and CeeCee, being true entrepreneurial types—"

"You mean normal witches."

I rolled my eyes. "Even more entrepreneurial than normal. Anyway, they had this idea of a one-stop shop. So instead of dealing in innovation and custom orders, which is a more typical path for witches, they're a convenience shop."

"In a thrift store."

I patted his knee. "That's right, in a thrift store. Although they prefer 'vintage.'"

"Got it," Ben said. But when we pulled up to the little old house with the peeling paint and limited parking, Ben said, "Vintage? I really think this place is more thrift than vintage."

"Wait till you see the inside." Though I hadn't a clue if inside was any better. I'd only heard from

CeeCee about the shop. I hadn't made time to visit in person yet.

"Hmm. Not that I'm knocking thrift stores—that's where we got your sweet patio set—but the run-down vibe says thrift more than vintage."

So far, I couldn't argue with him. Chipped and peeling paint did not bode well, though it really was a darling house.

Not two feet inside the door and we were mobbed by two enthusiastic witches.

"So good to see you," and "Finally! I'm so glad you made it!"

Bernard spoke and CeeCee bubbled over on top of him. He didn't seem to mind.

After Ben and I had extended our congratulations, I asked, "So business has been slow?" How could I not? Their greeting had been a little over the top. They seemed desperate for company.

"No." Bernard ran a hand through his already mussed hair. "Crazy. Insanely busy."

"Yeah," CeeCee agreed, while bouncing on her toes. "We haven't even had time to paint the exterior. I think we should hire painters, but Bernard insists we can do it ourselves." She narrowed her eyes at him and pointed. "Let's see what these guys think."

Without blinking, I said, "No comment."

Ben, wise man that he is, said nothing.

"See!" CeeCee poked Bernard in the chest. "They think it looks terrible."

"No, they're both too smart to insert themselves in the middle of a couple's dispute. Aren't you, guys?" Bernard smirked at us. If I had to guess, Bernard knew exactly how terrible the place looked and wasn't in any hurry to fix it. Business was good and he got to push CeeCee's buttons, win-win.

"Anyway." I looked around the shop for the first time and grinned. It was cool. With just a glance, I spotted an art deco dresser next to a 1960s wedding gown hanging from an unknown era coat stand, as well as what looked like some pretty cool original art. Grinning, I turned back to CeeCee. "Amazing place, but we're here because we need to know where to get salamander food."

"Ah, well, that's in the back room." She pointed to a hallway and ushered us ahead of her. Bernard stayed behind to man the shop as the rest of us continued to the back. We passed two open doors, each room full of artfully displayed goods, but then we reached one marked private. She reached around me and tapped the knob. "Go ahead."

I opened the door to find the largest magical pantry I'd ever seen. Even Camille's was only the size of her mudroom. Bernard and CeeCee had chosen the master bedroom for their stash of "special" goods, and then they'd lined the walls with shelves. Two long, tall tables were centered in the room. One held more jars, stones, charms, and gadgets. The other appeared to be a cluttered prep table.

"Wow." I spun around a full 360 degrees and then said again, "Wow. It's really cool."

"Uh-huh." The click of the door pulled my attention back to CeeCee, who was leaning against it. "So what exactly do you have to do with fire salamanders? Does this have anything to do with Alistair's death?"

She would jump immediately to the right conclusion. CeeCee was no fool.

"Just between us?" I asked with a serious look.

"Puh-lease. Of course. Now spill." Her eyes opened wide. "What scoop do you have?"

"Let's just say that we're looking into Alistair's *supposed* death."

She gasped. "That sneaky little jerk. And poor Marge." Eyes narrowing in suspicion, she said, "It'll have something to do with shady business dealings. I bet you a pouch of Vulcan powder."

"What's Vulcan powder?" I asked.

CeeCee winked. "What you just asked for. You

sprinkle it on the crickets before you feed them to your salamander. Only if you want him to belch flames, though."

I choked back a laugh. But I couldn't help it—a giggle or two slipped out. "Are you kidding me?"

"With the belching? Not even a little. It's actually much more predictable than you'd think. Fire salamanders aren't actually salamanders, and the little dudes belch a lot. Sprinkle some Vulcan powder on a few crickets, let him gorge himself, then startle him, and bam! Flames like you wouldn't believe."

"That's, uh..." Ben couldn't even finish the thought.

"Yep, sweetie. It's weird, even in the magical world of super strange." Turning to CeeCee, I asked, "What's in Vulcan powder?"

Serious in a flash, CeeCee said, "That's proprietary. But you know what's not proprietary? Who's been buying it lately. That fanged freak bought his own Vulcan powder. Does he think we don't talk?"

"You're kidding me." We couldn't be so lucky... could we? "Alistair bought Vulcan powder from you."

"He did. And I wouldn't have thought twice about it if you hadn't come in blathering about sala-

manders. It has"—she cleared her throat delicately
—"other uses."

I snorted. CeeCee wasn't usually so circumspect,
so I jabbed Ben in the ribs and said, "Cover your
virgin ears, honey."

Ben shook his head and headed for the door. "I'll
join Bernard up front. We can talk exterior paint."

At the words "exterior paint," CeeCee put her
hand over her heart. "Your guy is a sweetheart, isn't
he?" When I nodded, she said, "He's so perfect for
you. I never really got you and Alex as a couple.
Anyway, so, about that powder. Vulcan was the god
of fire and the forge. Think metal and hammering
and sex. 'Nuff said."

"Are you telling me that Alistair came in looking
for a gentleman's"—I glanced downward—
"pick-me-up?"

"More a lengthener, hardener, and, ah, stamina
increaser."

Thinking back on the few instances I'd met him,
I just couldn't picture it. "And he made that clear
when he bought it?"

"Crystal." She moved to the worktable and
started digging around a pile of what looked like
odds and ends. "I should have known when he was
so open that something hinky was afoot. No man

likes to admit that he's less than adequate in that department."

"If you're willing to make a statement to Cornelius, I think it will go a long way in proving Marge innocent."

She pulled a piece of parchment from the pile she'd been rummaging in and began to scribble. "What would make it even more obvious that she's innocent would be Alistair's miraculous recovery from death. Do you think there's any chance of finding him?"

"Alex is on it."

She raised her eyebrows. If she found it odd that I still worked with my ex on occasion, she didn't say. She gestured to the document, and I quickly read through the statement she'd written. When I nodded my approval, she folded and sealed it. Handing it to me, she said, "I'll contact Cornelius to let him know I've provided my official testimony to you, but that I will gladly come into headquarters and testify in person if necessary."

I wasn't a big hugger—excluding Ben, who could have all the hugs he wanted—but this was a hug moment.

CeeCee wrapped her arms around me, squeezed hard, and let go. "Go save your dragon."

With her statement clutched in my fingers, I followed CeeCee out of the best magical pantry ever. I'd take a page out of her book and create one of my own someday.

"You ladies get everything sorted?" Ben asked. He was leaning on the counter and Bernard was behind it. They looked thick as thieves.

"All good." I'd tell Ben all about Alistair's supposed sexual deficiencies in the car. I wasn't sure exactly what was in that powder that it both turned a salamander into a fire-belching beast and a man into a cross between the Energizer Bunny and Casanova. I wasn't sure I really wanted to know.

"Come back soon," CeeCee said with a cheery wave. "If you need anything, anything at all, you know where to come."

I snickered. Given what we'd been discussing, I knew exactly what she meant. "Thanks, all the same. I think we're good."

CeeCee winked, and I pulled Ben out of the store before he realized I'd just semipublicly proclaimed my sexual satisfaction.

15

"W**e have problems," I told Ben. He was driving us back to the funeral home at my request. "Other than having not a single suspect, someone—possibly Alistair—purchasing a salamander the day before the body was crisped, and Alistair purchasing the necessary foodstuffs to produce a fire-belching salamander, we've got nothing."

"You've said before how much Alex and Cornelius dislike circumstantial evidence." Ben rubbed his neck. "If Alex finds Alistair—"

"That's highly unlikely." Seeing Ben's expression, I said, "Okay, not highly. Alex is pretty amazing at his job. But it's unlikely."

"So why are we headed back the funeral home? You have something in mind."

I scrubbed my hands across my face and growled. "Ugh. I don't know what else to do. I'm going to beg Marge to give up her baby daddy's location. I'm hoping we can get a sample from him to prove that the damage to the corpse was inflicted by some other creature. I really don't see us catching a salamander anytime soon. I wouldn't know where to start. Even the magical creature whizz kid said it takes time."

Ben shifted in the driver's seat. "I don't see Marge giving up her mate. Not even if he was just a sperm donor. What if the tide turns and they go after him instead of Marge because he's accessible?"

"Yeah, I get it. That's exactly why I won't ask her to come forward to give a sample of her fire. But I have to ask anyway."

"And then? When she says no? What about another look at the body? You were rushed before. Maybe now, knowing that it isn't Alistair—or probably isn't Alistair—you can look for evidence pointing to the true identity of the corpse."

And that only made me feel worse. If he was a young vamp, he might not have cut ties with his family yet. There could be people out there missing him, worrying about him.

"Yeah. We'll talk to Marge and then take another look at the body." I didn't know what I might find, but Ben wasn't wrong. I *had* been rushed. "Oh, no. I forgot to mask the explosion of magic in the field next to the funeral home."

"I'm sure it's fine. If no one's been by, then no one's had a chance to see it."

Except, wouldn't you know, when we arrived back at the funeral home, someone was waiting for us. A vampire in a snit.

Tall, thin, brunette, and ridiculously gorgeous, a woman stood at the front door, waiting impatiently. And when I say impatiently, I mean with glowing red eyes.

Other than the differences in their figures, there was a striking similarity between this woman and Lisette. The dark, glossy hair, the sculpted cheekbones, porcelain skin, and full lips. I'd bet she had chocolatey brown eyes when they weren't bleeding red.

She had to be Odette.

When she spoke, my suspicion was confirmed. She had more than a trace of a French accent. "I have spoken with Lisette. We do not think Alistair is dead."

It seemed Alistair had a very specific type. I really couldn't get over the similarities.

"Oh?" I asked, with just a touch of curiosity. Ben assumed a neutral expression and remained silent.

"Yes. We think that Alistair, he is alive. What do you say?" She waved her hand wildly as she searched for the word. "It is the setup."

Yeah, her accent was definitely stronger than Lisette's, because it took me a second to process what she was saying and garner her meaning. "You think that Alistair has faked his death."

Much as I tried to make it sound like the thought hadn't even crossed my mind, I clearly failed.

She narrowed her eyes and stabbed a finger at me. "You. You know this. I see your lie in the eyes." When I didn't reply, she threw her hands in the air. "Alistair, he is impossible! He tries to end with Lisette, but she makes the goo-goo eyes and he cannot say no. Now he tried to end with me, then change his mind, and poof, he is gone."

Ben shook his head. "You think Alistair faked his death to break up with you and Lisette?"

"No. I do not say this." She pursed her lips. "The one happens, then the other. But we are not the reason. No." Again, she stabbed the air violently, but this time she wasn't pointing specifically at me. "It is the business. Always with the money and the business. I have money. Lisette, she has money."

Her agitation was making me nervous. Perhaps if I could convince her to come inside and have a seat, she'd calm down. "Would you like to come in so we can discuss Alistair and his—"

"No. No, I will not go inside, in your house for dead bodies."

I caught the hint of a smile twitching at the corners of Ben's mouth. He better stop it, or I'd be laughing at the most inappropriate of times. And while Odette sounded like a woman who'd been wronged by her man, she was a *vampire* who'd been wronged by her man.

Ill-timed laughter was not advisable.

One deep, calming breath later, I said, "You think that Alistair might have faked his death so that he could burn this identity and create another."

It was common practice in our world. The enhanced lived longer lives. Some, like the witches, only marginally so. But a vampire might assume a dozen or more identities in their life-time. That said, records were kept and memories were long in the enhanced community. If Alistair was trying to ditch his identity not only in the mundane world but also in the enhanced community, substituting a burned body for his own wasn't the worst idea.

It just wasn't the absolute best. And it was outright nasty for him to have set up Marge as the fall guy.

Ben finally spoke up. "If Alistair were still alive, where would he be?"

I could kiss him. In all the fluster of Odette's dramatics, that most essential of questions had evaded me. I leaned forward as I waited for her response.

She tapped a perfectly manicured nail against her full lower lip. "I do not know." But she continued to tap away at her lip.

How did she do that without smudging her oh-so-perfect lipstick?

"Ah! I have eeet!" Her accent thickened in her enthusiasm. "Ze farmhouse." She looked me up and down. "I go only once, many months ago, but I remember ze way. You will find him and bring him back?"

Why were these gorgeous, successful women so into Alistair? He was more than passable looking, but the man was a grade-A jerk. He'd dumped them in the worst possible way, and yet... I mentally shrugged. "Sure. No promises, but I might have someone who can make that happen."

Odette practically purred. "Alex, yes? He is... How do you say? Lickable."

"Um, I'm not sure that's what you—"

"Yes, he is." Ben nudged me gently. "Where is the farmhouse?"

Odette proceeded to give us very specific directions to a very remote house in the countryside, southwest of town.

"He will be there. He will wait until the dragon, she is dead, the body, it is buried, and the hubbub, it is over." She pronounced "hubbub" with the accent on the wrong part of the word, which again almost made me laugh.

But this was good intel. Great insight into the jerkface who'd framed Marge. All desire to laugh died. We thanked her politely for her help—one shouldn't be too profuse in thanking vamps—and then watched her walk to her car.

Ben handed me his phone as soon as her door had slammed.

"Alex," I said when he picked up, "I don't suppose you've found our guy?"

A grumbly growl was my answer.

"That's all right. I have a hot tip for you. You're

going to need a pen and paper." Then I handed the phone to Ben, because his memory for directions was absurdly good.

Ben ended the call after repeating the directions and then listening to Alex read them back.

I thumped his chest. "You know what this means, right?"

He gave me a curious look, but had no response.

I couldn't help the huge smile that stretched across my face. "If she's right, if he's holed up in that old farmhouse, then we've got him—and he'll have been brought down by the very women he tried to ditch."

It was an immensely satisfying feeling to think that the women in Alistair's life, the ones he treated so poorly—because stringing along two women only to fake your death could hardly be called anything else—were the source of his ultimate failure. They were the ones who knew him best, and their intimate knowledge of Alistair had wrecked his plans.

I hoped.

If that body wasn't Alistair's and all of us hadn't taken a massive leap into crazy land.

"Lisette was the one who gave you all of the missing information that made you suspect he was still alive, and now Odette with his possible hiding place." He wrapped an arm around me and gave me a stout side-hug. "But you did all the best parts in the middle."

"Please. I don't need the runner-up award or sympathy points. If Marge evades punishment for a crime she didn't commit, if her eggling manages to hatch without complications, and if that nut Alistair fails to disappear into the distance and re-create himself, then I couldn't be happier."

The glow lasted about two minutes. That's when my bubble burst, and I realized the worst was yet to come.

Now Ben and I had to *wait*.

16

Waiting really wasn't my strong suit. I wouldn't say I was impatient, more that I liked to be doing. Fixing, solving, and acting were all so much easier than twiddling my thumbs.

If the body were still on the premises, I could have taken that second look. Even so, I still thought it was the smarter plan to have it secured at a safer, alternative location.

It was time to start looking at the funeral home's security, now that Ben was the official body disposal for all local enhanced corpses. Definitely if I was ever going to do another magical autopsy. Preferable a *complete* one, rather than the slipshod quick look that I'd had of our not-Alistair corpse.

But whether it was the quickie kind or a more thorough version, magical autopsies were conducted on bodies that had died in questionable circumstances. That made them evidence. Yeah, more security was definitely going on my short list of to-dos.

But I was currently occupied with a completely different set of to-dos.

I'd decided to do some bookkeeping in Ben's office, because it was better than staring at the walls waiting for Alex to call with news of a captured Alistair. What I'd actually done was doodle a list of impossibilities.

Find one small fire salamander who likely was no longer living or had been turned loose to live his best life in the Texas hill country.

Connect Alistair to the purchase of that Salamander, which required me to...

Find the pet store owner in Vegas and convince him to testify against Alistair.

Assuming the big bad vamp had bought the salamander himself.

So many ifs.

A tap on the office door startled me. Ben leaned in the doorway with his arms crossed. "Alex is doing what he does best. Let him take this guy into custody."

"If Alistair's still alive," I replied. "If he's at the farmhouse, if we're not completely off base with our theories. On the bright side, I did ask Cornelius to check into any missing young vampires. He's getting a status on any vamp under a decade."

"You called Cornelius?"

"Don't sound so utterly shocked. He's not that terrifying."

Ben didn't look convinced.

"Okay, fine. He is a little scary. But if the corpse is young—and the lack of residual magic implies that's the case—then the victim may still have living family. It felt wrong to sit on that information."

Ben had a funny look on his face. He walked to his desk—basically *my* desk at this point, with all the admin I'd taken over—and hugged me from behind.

He added a quick kiss to the side of my neck, before whispering into my ear, "I love you."

I frowned. "Because I called Cornelius."

He chuckled, gave me another squeeze, then stood up. "No, I just love you. But I also love that you care about the victim and his family enough to call Cornelius."

Since I hadn't had the time to complete a full autopsy and I'd known it would come up, it had been an even more difficult call to make. Cornelius was bad enough. But a Cornelius who was disappointed in my work?

Surprisingly, he hadn't said much at all about the fact that I could only give him a preliminary report on the body, and he agreed without hesitation to check into the status of the handful of young vamps in the area.

I didn't get a chance to explain any of that to Ben. First, my neck prickled, and not in the sexy, good way. And then, a split second later, a vaguely familiar voice said, "Aren't you two adorable."

Alistair.

I really did need to upgrade our security.

He stood in the doorway to the office where Ben had only moments earlier.

"Can I help you?" Ben asked in a tone only slightly less polite than his usual.

Oops. Ben hadn't met Alistair before.

Alistair gave Ben a dismissive look, then focused all of his pissed-off-vampire, bleeding-red-eyed gaze on me. "Where's the body?"

Which made me smile. A genuine, ear-to-ear smile. "Not here."

Looked like I'd done something right.

Also—Alistair was alive!

That right there was enough to make a dragon-loving witch happy. And this dragon-loving witch needed a win, given the impossible to-do list I'd been drafting. No more looking for a fire salamander that would never be found, for instance.

"You're an incompetent, magicless, loser. You were supposed to have already buried the body." That vile bit of nastiness was directed at Ben.

I squeezed his arm. Reassurance that I had our vampire problem in hand...which I didn't. Vampires were fast. Sure, a lot of the things that killed humans killed them, but you had to catch them. Preferably before they ripped your throat out. And also not be susceptible to any powers of persuasion they might have.

Fun times.

But then I couldn't help being struck by the ludicrousness of Alistair's response.

I had a pretty good idea what would have happened to the corpse after Ben had interred it. Vanished. Stolen by a dead man who wasn't dead in an attempt to cover his tracks. And somehow Ben was incompetent for...what? Thwarting Alistair's plans?

And there was the evidence he'd left behind: a burned vampire body that anyone other than

Clarice would never mistake as an old vamp; buying the salamander food himself; and if my guess was right, buying the actual salamander himself.

Alistair really wasn't very good at all this planning and killing himself off stuff. I was starting to get a picture of exactly how bad at business he might be.

Which sparked an idea. Well, Alistair's fragile ego, plus his incompetence, and Will, the funeral home bookkeeper's, recent addiction to Yankee Candles all sparked an idea.

"You bought the salamander food from CeeCee and Bernard yourself. I mean, seriously? Who's the incompetent one again?" I smiled at him. I went with the pity smile, because it was bound to make him the angriest.

The words made his eyes bleed red, but it was my smile that had his fangs coming out.

Which was just fine with me, so long as he didn't pounce quite yet—and also didn't notice that I'd cracked open the shallow top drawer that ran underneath the center of the desk.

"And I'm waiting on proof that you purchased the salamander. Should be here any minute." From the look on Alistair's face, I'd guessed right that he hadn't sent a henchman. So I kept rolling—and also poked my fingers inside the drawer, hunting for the weapon I knew was stashed there. "How did you even think a young vamp corpse could ever pass as you? You're, like, a hundred years old or something."

And that last blow, my wildly inaccurate guess as to his age, gave me the lapse in concentration that I needed. Ancient vamps had the biggest egos.

"Clarice should have—"

Too late, Alistair saw the flames coming at him.

He'd wanted the world to believe he'd been deep fried, so who was I to naysay him?

17

_____

"It was crazy," Ben said. "It was like one of those circus acts where they breathe fire. Or, no, it was more like on TV when an action hero turns hairspray and a lighter into a flamethrower. Actually, a little of both. It was so cool."

I had no idea that my honey was so bloodthirsty. Then again, he was on his third beer, and Alistair was a deeply unsympathetic individual—one who was alive and able to heal his burns, since they hadn't been made by a dragon or a fire salamander.

Alex, Camille, Bernard, CeeCee, Cornelius, and Natalie were all seated in a circle around two coolers and a grill outside the funeral home warehouse, listening to Ben recount our Adventures in Conquering Alistair.

He made it sound much more interesting than the reality, which had been painful (for Alistair), disturbing (for me), and shocking (for Ben).

But there was a happy ending for Marge. With Alistair outed as the big ol' liar pants that he was, she was safe from the false justice the vamp horde would have demanded, and the eggling was safe from discovery by the magical masses.

Alistair wasn't sitting in a jail cell. The Society didn't have a jail, just the option to execute criminals, and Alistair's crimes hadn't risen to that level, per Cornelius. But Alistair had been shamed in the community. He'd have a heck of a hard time escaping the rumors of his actions, so even moving to a new city wasn't going to help him much. And he had moved. Immediately.

That was the closest to justice we'd get, and I'd decided to be satisfied with it.

Besides, there were more important events afoot today. I refused to waste my energy on anything as unworthy as resentment toward Alistair on a day like today.

Ben and I had invited a trusted few friends to grill and drinks beers—except for Natalie, who had grumbled when we'd shove a soda in her hand—

and, more importantly, to celebrate the hatching of an egg.

Since we couldn't exactly lurk in the shadows of the warehouse, we'd set up camp outside its doors.

"Well, go on then." CeeCee nudged my foot. "Tell us how you did it."

"Ben might be exaggerating a teeny bit. It wasn't all that exciting." I stretched out my feet in front of me. These camp chairs were surprisingly comfortable. "I happened to be working on a little amplification spell. I thought that the spell, plus the lighter, plus a nice gusty breath aimed at Alistair might have the desired effect."

"By desired effect," Alex said, "what she means is charred vampire."

There were snickers and chuckles around the circle. No one was saving any sympathy for Alistair. I felt a little sick about having hurt someone, but then I'd remind myself that Alistair hadn't been paying a social call at the time and had likely planned to harm—perhaps even kill—Ben and me.

"Our bookkeeper started burning candles in the office about a month ago, and he keeps a lighter in the desk," Ben provided with a proud grin. "But that wasn't the tricky part."

"Yes, please do tell us about the tricky part."

Cornelius had the same trick of smiling without actually smiling that Alex had.

He seemed amused by my fire stunt. Thank goodness. I didn't want to be on Cornelius's bad side.

I was glad he wasn't showing any signs of holding a grudge. After having him chase down all the newly turned vamps, it turned out that the corpse wasn't a vampire at all. Alistair admitted to having purchased a body roughly the same height and weight as himself. But Cornelius hadn't uttered a single word of complaint about wasted effort. I was counting myself lucky that Cornelius hadn't charged me for the time spent welfare checking the new vamps. I knew exactly how tight he could be with Society resources.

"The tricky part was distracting him enough to catch him unaware."

Cornelius nodded. "Witches aren't known for their preternatural speed, unlike vampires."

"Nicely done," Alex said as he lifted his beer can in my direction. Unlike Ben, Alex was still sipping his first.

Natalie disappeared inside the warehouse to check on Marge as the conversation moved into the realm of what would have happened if I hadn't managed the tricky part and Alistair had pulled a dodge and weave that would have saved him from the flames. I tuned it out as I kept an eye on the warehouse door.

She was only gone a minute or two.

"Should be soon, but not quite yet," Natalie announced when she returned.

The moody teenager had been surprisingly helpful with Marge. Her significantly improved attitude might have something to do with the once-in-a-lifetime invitation she'd received. An egg-hatching event could make the grumpiest of souls a little brighter.

I was glad Marge had found a way to ask us to invite Natalie. That had been a serious bunch of charades. After that, adding the rest of the crew to the list hadn't been nearly so cumbersome.

This was a happy occasion, no doubt, but there was one piece of the puzzle that hadn't been solved. Alistair hadn't known the name of the man whose body had been burned. Kawolski Funeral Home was responsible for laying him to rest, and we didn't know who he was. He deserved a proper, respectful burial. One with a marker that named the soul resting in the ground below it.

Ben stopped and pulled me into his arms. "We'll figure out who he is."

I looked up into his kind eyes. He knew me so well. "Sorry. You're right, and now isn't the time to be dwelling on it, anyway. I can't believe that I'm about to see a baby dragon."

We had to wait until the little baby had fully imprinted on Momma Marge. She'd threatened to singe the door if anyone cracked it open too soon after the eggling hatched.

"You're allowed to feel more than one emotion. You're allowed to feel however you feel. But we'll take care of it." He kissed my neck. "We'll even ask Alex to help."

And now he was just messing with me.

I poked him in the side, and he picked me up and threw me over his shoulder. Yeah, I knew better than to poke his tickle spot in public. He hated that he was ticklish.

And that was when it happened. Thrown over my boyfriend's shoulder, I got an upside-down view of the door to the warehouse disappearing in a puff of ash and smoke.

Rather than shouts of concern, there were whoops of excitement, mostly from Natalie. Mamma Marge wouldn't accidentally incinerate a door, but Natalie had told us that the baby's first breath would be a ball of fire.

"Our baby dragon is just fine," she hollered.

"Watch out, everyone," Bernard said. "I read that they can get two or three fireballs out before they calm down."

Supposedly, baby dragons let loose that little burst of flame when they hatched, but then didn't have any fire for days after. Or so Natalie said.

I kissed Ben on the cheek after he set me back down on my feet and gave him a smile that was filled with all the joy I was feeling. "We get to meet a baby dragon! Don't you just love this?"

"Yes. Yes, I do." Funny thing, Ben wasn't looking at the smoking door. He was looking at me.

***

THANK you for reading *Tickle the Dragon's Tail*! I hope you've been enjoying Star and Ben's witchy adventures. Find out what happens when Camille, Star's mentor, decides that Star and Ben would be good petsitters for Star's favorite grumpy feline.

Pick up *Twinkles Takes a Holiday* to read how Ben and Star try to clear Twinkles's name for a crime they *think* he didn't commit.

Turn the page for an excerpt from *Twinkles Takes a Holiday*...

EXCERPT: TWINKLES TAKES A HOLIDAY

Prologue: *The Cat's Meow (Twinkles)*
My life is pretty fabulous.
No cooking—ever.

A maid who cleans at least daily.

Soft, high spots perfectly placed to catch luscious streams of sunlight.

A personal servant (or human...you say to-may-to, I say to-mah-to) to stroke my back and scratch under my chin.

But...

Daily catering gets old when it's always the same old canned food.

Bathrooms should be tidied *frequently*. Is it too much to ask for morning, noon, and night service?

A bed can be soft and perfectly placed, but it's

still located within a house. What is "house" but another word for cage?

And a human who gives scratches is all well and good when that human is actually *home*. My human happens to be gallivanting in parts distant.

Sometimes, I just want to be human. Have two legs, stride around like I own the place. Use my opposable thumbs to rule the world.

Little things.

I'm not asking all that much.

But I never thought my wish for humanity would come to fruition.

I wouldn't say the message on the answering phone surprised me. Or the very particular instructions to delete the message. Or even the package that followed.

Chapter 1: Mostly a Cat (Star)

Where's the cat?" A note of near-panic entered my boyfriend Ben's voice. "Star, where is that evil maniac?"

Twinkles wasn't evil.

Self-interested, yes. Completely unconcerned with pleasing the humans in his life, also yes. Intent on actively causing drama or even harm...probably not?

My mentor Camille had placed a lot of faith in

Ben and me when she'd left her precious cat in our care. Granted, no one else could be trusted. Certainly not a human.

Twinkles was a cat...mostly. He was the primary reason I hesitated to adopt a dog or a cat or even a hamster. I didn't want a mostly-cat cat or a mostly-dog dog. And as a witch, I rolled the dice when I took a pet into my household.

Most witch pets were just pets. Ninety-nine-point-nine percent of them, in fact. But occasionally, for reasons unknown, a witch's pet became something more. Just my luck that the cat I was pet-sitting happened to be one of the point-one percent.

If there hadn't been hints concerning his true nature previous to his twenty-fifth birthday, reaching that advanced age looking no more than any other cat of three or four had sealed the deal.

But there had definitely been hints.

He understood everything. Cats were clever, but Twinkles got nuance. And since I'd been inside the little so-and-so's head, I knew for a fact he understood us very, very well.

Twinkles was probably how the whole concept of familiars got started back in the dark days of witch burnings. Not Twinkles personally—obviously; he was twenty-five—but witch-affected pets like Twinkles.

It wasn't just understanding humans. These witch-affected animals could problem-solve and complete complex tasks. Twinkles, for example, had constructed a ladder of pillows, books, and a footstool to climb up to the thermostat and increase the temperature by ten degrees.

Oh, and there was that one time that Camille took him out on a leash. Why she thought he'd be safe within five miles of a traveling children's petting zoo, I didn't know. That poor reindeer... The story had made the rounds at the time. Twinkles had been a pseudo-celebrity in the magic community for at least a week or so.

And all of that without opposable thumbs. Add hands, and there would be a mice-chasing, sunbathing, sudoku-loving sociopath running around creating more chaos than a gaggle of dehydrated vampires.

The more I considered the foibles of witch-affected pets, the more I had to wonder if it was purely a cat problem. I had a difficult time envisioning a dog with Twinkles' particular condition.

Truly, the point was moot. Dog, cat, hamster—it didn't matter. After the mess of the past few days, no way was I interested in adding a furry companion to the fold.

Ben and I were less than fully prepared for the care and feeding of Twinkles the mostly-cat, and that had put both of us off the idea of pets.

How unprepared we both were had just become disturbingly clear, because Twinkles was AWOL.

Ben could check under the sofa five times and peer into every shadowy corner of Camille's house, but he wouldn't find him. I could *feel* that Twinkles was absent.

"So, Ben?" I rocked back on my heels and waited for him to stand back up. He'd gone for a sixth look under the sofa. Not a good sign, since Ben was usually the calm one of the two of us. Super chill, my boyfriend—except for now.

He brushed his hands on his jeans, but then he saw the look on my face and started backing up. "I don't like that look. That's a bad look."

Without asking for details, he headed straight for the liquor cabinet.

Not that Ben was a big drinker. He was usually the designated driver and perfectly happy to cart my lightweight self around. But these last few days had been...difficult. Trying. Borderline disastrous.

On the plus side, I had definitive proof that Ben

was head over heels, completely gone for me. No way would a guy who wasn't completely in love with me put up with the feline shenanigans of this last week.

He'd been scratched, peed on, bitten (in a rather sensitive area), and locked in a kitchen pantry. And that was what I'd witnessed firsthand. I suspected Twinkles of several other less-than-admirable acts, but Ben wasn't talking.

The day before yesterday, when Ben had come home looking shell-shocked, I'd decided no more unaccompanied trips to Camille's house to check on the fluffy menace. Strength in numbers and all that.

"There is no telling what that little ball of fluff will get up to if he's escaped the house." Ben added a few cubes to the seltzer water he'd poured. It looked like we weren't quite to the point of booze. "How so much nasty can live in such a cute, furry body, I do not understand."

"I'll drive if you want to, you know, drown your sorrows in apple pucker."

He laughed, thankfully. That was what I'd been going for. I hated seeing my guy all twisted up, especially over witchy goings-on.

"Keeping a clear head is probably a better choice, but I'm glad you've got my back—in case the apple pucker starts calling my name. Wait, why does Camille have apple pucker?"

I gave him the don't-ask face, then grabbed a pen. Better to brainstorm places Twinkles would be likely to go than revisit past (bad, very bad) alcohol decisions. Apple pucker had definitely been one of my Ben-free, girly nights. There had been a lot of pucker shots (apple and watermelon), a lot of Lifetime movies, and a little crying.

Right...Twinkles. What did Twinkles do all day long? I made a quick note to check on the neighbor two doors down with the pretty Persian and the neighbor directly behind with the barking dogs.

Ben leaned over my shoulder and read my notes aloud. "I'm thinking revenge before love."

The scowl on his face prompted me to ask, "Any chance you want to tell me what happened day before yesterday? I know he's gone a little crazy with the scratching and the biting—"

"Oh, it was more than scratching and biting." Even though he was a redhead, Ben didn't blush much. The perk of being a generally chill guy who also had a lot of experience dealing with other people's strong emotions. Being a funeral director meant a lot of tears came his way. And yet he was blushing now.

But if he didn't want to talk about it, that was his prerogative.

"You have anything for the list?" I asked, firmly shelving the Twinkles-Ben mystery for now.

"He has a ridiculous love of pizza. Add that local pizza place he likes so much to the list."

That place was a good six or seven miles away, maybe more, and didn't deliver. "You do remember that he's incredibly lazy."

"But also clever. That cat is *not* normal."

"Very true."

And with that in mind, we came up with a list of places to check, regardless of distance from Camille's home. It was about an even split of things we knew Twinkles loved (restaurants, primarily, but also the Persian a few houses down), places he would find entertaining (the yarn store, though he tried to hide his string obsession), and the people he would like to make miserable (the neighbors with the barking dogs topped the list).

"I vote the two neighbors first," Ben said, "and then the pizza place, then we make a circle and hit everything on the list, closest first."

"Let's do it." I was thinking, *How bad could it be? He's a cat.*

But I refrained from articulating such dangerous

thoughts. If I spoke the words aloud, that devilish beast, Murphy's law, would surely swoop in and show me exactly how wrong I was.

Pick up your copy of *Twinkles Takes a Holiday* to keep reading about Twinkles' adventure on the town! Spoiler: Star and Ben do their best to ruin his fun ;-)

ABOUT THE AUTHOR

When Cate's not tapping away at her keyboard or in deep contemplation of her next fanciful writing project, she's sweeping up hairy dust bunnies and watching British mysteries.

She lives with her pack of pointers and hounds, some of whom make appearances in her books. She's worked as an attorney, a dog trainer, and in various other positions, but writer is the hands-down winner. She hopes you enjoy reading her stories as much as she loves writing them!

Printed in Great Britain
by Amazon